FRESH
GIRL

FRESH GIRL

Jaïra Placide

WENDY
LAMB
BOOKS

Published by
Wendy Lamb Books
an imprint of
Random House Children's Books
a division of Random House, Inc.
1540 Broadway
New York, New York 10036

Visit us on the Web! www.randomhouse.com/teens
Educators and librarians, for a variety of teaching tools, visit us at
www.randomhouse.com/teachers

Library of Congress Cataloging-in-Publication Data

Placide, Jaïra.
    Fresh girl / Jaïra Placide.
      p. cm.
    Summary: After having been sent, at a very young age, from New York to live with her grandmother in Haiti, fourteen-year-old Mardi returns to join her parents and try to shape a new life in Brooklyn.
    ISBN 0-385-90035-X (lib. bdg.)–ISBN 0-385-32753-6
    1. Haitian Americans–Juvenile fiction. [1. Haitian Americans–Fiction. 2. Haiti–Fiction. 3. Brooklyn (New York, N.Y.)–Fiction. 4. Grandmothers–Fiction.] I. Title.

PZ7.P695 Fr 2002
[Fic]–dc21   2001032427

The text of this book is set in 11-point Baskerville.

Book design by Melissa J Knight

Manufactured in the United States of America

January 2002

10 9 8 7 6 5 4 3

BVG

Pou maman-m

('Via? 'Via?)

*

To

My Mother,

whose life was a long labor of patience, commitment,

and love to her family and friends,

this book is gratefully inscribed

by

Her Daughter

I am good.

The lion's lips are complete; so are the monkey's tail and the kangaroo's legs. I'm making this, me. It's me who's putting together all the animals in the kingdom. I put together a 250-piece puzzle in less than an hour. And the lights aren't even on. My legs are cold on the broken-tiled bathroom floor.

I look at the glow-in-the-dark Mickey Mouse watch my father found in his taptap van last week. It's two o'clock in the morning. I'm tired but I don't want to go back to sleep. What if I dream about the soldiers again? What if I dream about Ike at school? What if I wake up dead?

I get up and wash my hands. I scrub and scrub with the Brillo pad. The backs of my hands hurt, but I feel better.

I push back the yellow plastic window curtains to let more street light shine on my puzzle on the floor, but it's missing. The lion in the picture is gone. I'm scared now because I know I'm the only one in the bathroom and the only one awake in the apartment. I really don't want the lion to eat up my family.

Then I hear a growl from behind the shower curtains. I move slowly to the light switch and turn it on.

The growl is louder.

I move toward the shower curtains, mumbling the Act of Contrition. Grandmère taught me to say the prayer so God will forgive me for all my sins, so God will protect me from all my sins.

I pull apart the curtains.

Nothing there.

I go back to the puzzle and find the lion smiling at me once again.

"Do you smell something, Mardi?" Jilline Hunter sits across from me, sniffing the air. We're in English class waiting for the teacher to come.

"Uh, no," I say, praying that no one thinks it's me. I made sure I washed my underarms three times before I left my house this morning. "I don't smell any *ting*."

Oh, no, my accent.

"You don't smell any *thing*!" This comes from Ike, one aisle over, breathing fire on everyone's back. "You's one dumb island girl. When you gonna learn how to be talking English right?"

I open my English writing notebook, Malice. In stories my grandmother used to tell me, Malice is the clever one who always gets away with his tricks. I write: *If I were God for a day I would* never *let Ike be born.* I underline "never" twice.

Then I notice Pierre LeBalle several desks in front of me, secretly eating a bag of onion-cheese potato chips.

Pierre, again. Always making the rest of us Haitians look bad with her mountain-folk ways.

"So, Frenchie." Ike jumps in my face. "You got HBO today, huh? You got Haitian Body Odor today?"

Everyone's looking at me, including Santos Amorez and The Mildred Rodriguez, the best-looking people in all of Flatbush, Brooklyn. The Mildred Rodriguez and some girls around her giggle, giggle, giggle like cartoon witches.

My heart is thumping in my throat.

Jilline speaks for me: "Leave her alone, Isaac!"

My heart slides back in its place.

"Who you, her mama?"

"If I was I'd knock your nappy head back into the third grade!" Now Jilline's accent comes out, but hers is American, and Southern, and angry.

Ike smiles and leans back as if surprised. "Calm down, girl. No one wanna fight. I'm just playin'. You don't mind, right, Mardi?"

Do crocodiles bite? But I shake my head. I look at Santos and breathe out. He's staring back at me, but I can't tell if he's with Ike or Jilline.

Mrs. Orlando finally rushes in. "So sorry to be late but I— Everybody better quiet down or there will be plenty for you to write about."

The class gets quiet real quick.

"I have your exams back from the first part of *To Kill a Mockingbird*." She holds up the papers. "Many of you have not done your reading, which explains your very creative answers. So at the end of this period you're getting a makeup test."

The class groans.

"For those of you who did well, this will be extra credit. Mardi?" Mrs. Orlando is smiling at me. "You have the highest score again. Will you please hand these out?"

I slowly get up from my seat and take the papers. As Mrs. Orlando writes notes on the board, I give out the exams.

Pierre gets a 79.

Jilline a 72.

Santos and Mildred both get 68's.

Ike an 83.

And I get 100. I "accidentally" hand Ike, Santos, and The Mildred Rodriguez my paper. The dumb island girl rides again.

Mardi Desravines. In French my name means Tuesday *(Mardi)* of the ravines *(des ravines)*. Maman named me Mardi because I was born on a Tuesday. Thank God it wasn't a Wednesday because then my name would have been Mercredi. In English it sounds like a pain reliever. I was born in New York City, the first one of my family to be a natural citizen. Sometimes my mother and father call me *dènye-an,* "the last one," or "the one who was born here," as if those few words could sum me up when they introduce me.

They had me right after they came to New York looking for work, and when I was four years old, they sent me to Haiti to live with Grandmère Adda, my father's mother. That was when both my mother and father started working double shifts and there was no one to look after me anymore. Grandmère Adda told them to send me to her. She had a big house in Port-au-Prince and was also looking after my sister, Serina, who was eight at the time. Serina was born in Port-au-Prince and we had never met. I wasn't exactly dying to meet her.

One morning I woke up in New York and Maman's sausage and eggs were burning—and she was standing right in front of the stove, too. Maman and Papa both kept telling me I was going on a trip.

"Yeah! Di'neyland?"

"No."

"The park with water inside?"

"No."

"Puppy in the window?"

"No."

Hmm. "Di'neyland?"

They were extra nice to me that morning. My father let me sit on his lap to eat my breakfast. He kept saying how smart I was and how I would do well in something I'd be doing a long way from that day. My mother let me brush her hair and didn't snatch the brush from me when I accidentally hit her on the head with it. She kind of smiled and touched my chin; I thought I was in heaven.

Then we went to the airport. When it was time to get on the plane, I reached for my mother. But she put two pictures in my hand: one of her and my father, and the other of this old woman who was my grandmother. I knew something was up when they both kissed me. Why would they do that if we were going to be together?

One of my mother's friends walked up to us. She was a nice lady who came to our house sometimes. What was she doing there?

"Thank you so much, Madan Rose, for looking after Mardi on the plane," my mother told her. Madan Rose took my hand and began to lead me into the plane.

"You coming?" I called after my mother and father.

They looked at each other. "Be good," they said. "Tell your grandmother—"

I started to go back but Madan Rose pulled me away.

"Mardi!" my mother said. "Don't misbehave. Get on the plane and listen to what they tell you."

Okay, I said to myself. If you want me to go, I'll go. So I got on the plane without a fight. I wanted to show them I wasn't a big baby. I didn't cry; I went to sleep instead. When I woke up, I couldn't find my pictures. I asked Madan Rose but she didn't know where they were. I don't know why but I kept thinking she had taken them.

We landed in Port-au-Prince. This airport was different. I was outside when I got off the plane, and there was a long staircase from the plane to the ground.

There was sun.

I could smell something cooking, or burning, and the air felt like someone sighing.

I saw mountains all around.

I heard music: three men in white pants singing.

There were people clapping and waving on the roof of the airport. Madan Rose waved back and called out a name. She tried to take my hand but I wouldn't let her and ran down the steps.

We finally got our luggage and then I met my family for the first time. Grandmère was clapping like a church woman.

"Aaahhh, bravo! Saint Joseph!" she said. "Look at the sweet package from New York!"

I looked at my sister. Serina had big teeth and dimples. She kissed me and gave me her newest Barbie doll. My aunt wouldn't stop singing, and my uncle promised to take me swimming in some river.

Who were *they*?

We all got into a van and drove to Grandmère Adda's blue house. My uncle was driving, with Grandmère next to him. I was behind them, a small suitcase on my lap, in between Serina and my aunt. Serina kept playing with my hair, and my aunt had her hand on my shoulder.

"These barrettes are pretty," Serina said, "but I've got more at home."

"Aaahhh, leave the girl alone," Grandmère said. "Mardi, are you hungry?"

I shook my head but she gave me a banana anyway.

The house was as big as a cathedral. Serina took my hand, telling me we would sleep in the same room. She talked nonstop. After a while she sounded like a bee.

When we came to "our" room, I went straight to bed with my shoes and clothes on and pulled the covers over my head. I remember I stayed like that for a long time. I told them I was sick and my aunt said, "Sick for Mommy and Daddy?" I yelled at her, "No!" and pulled the covers up even farther.

Grandmère came with lots of food, Serina arranged all her dolls in front of me, and one time I think my aunt and uncle came in with music. But I wouldn't get out of bed. One night I saw them all by my bed looking down at me. I could have been dreaming. I remember it in pieces. I wished I could tell them that all I wanted was to go back home to where my mother and father were.

At recess I stand by myself in Taliaferro Junior High's courtyard; it's September so it's still warm and nice. I'm scratching a cut on my hand. When it opens again, I take a Band-Aid out of my pocket and cover it.

Taliaferro Junior High shares the yard with a connecting elementary school. I'm watching some fourth- and fifth-grade girls I know from church jump double Dutch. I'm not much bigger than they are—people think I'm eleven, not fourteen—so I walk up and tap this one skinny girl on the shoulder.

"Can I get a jump?"

She looks me up and down.

"I'll turn for it. Just a quick jump, please?"

"Awright," she finally says, "but you better not run off or try and get your other friends jumps. This game is closed after you."

I pop in the air the second I'm inside the rope. *Whoop! Whoop! Whoop! Whoop!* The rope makes its own sound and wind. It feels so good. I whisper in Créole:

Pim pim bo!	*Pim pim bo!*
Chire soulye, bo!	*Tear our shoes, bo!*
Sa pa di-n anyen, bo!	*Doesn't mean a thing to us, bo!*
Manman ap bay lòt, bo!	*Mother will give us more, bo!*
Papa achte lòt, bo!	*Papa will buy us more, bo!*
Pim pim bo!	*Pim pim bo!*

When I'm done, I turn for my jump like I promised.

"You jump and turn good," says the skinny girl. "You wanna play?"

I check to see if any other ninth graders are watching. Since we're in a far corner of the yard, I don't see any, but still, I'm too cool to be jumping rope. "I'll just turn for you."

I see Pierre LeBalle on the other side of the yard shooting basketball with this boy who just moved into our building. I think he's her cousin or something. He's good; he makes four baskets in a row. Pierre laughs and gets him in a headlock. She acts like such a boy. I'm not dying to be her friend, but at least when I'm with her, people don't mess with me. Pierre's a big girl and she fights like Mike Tyson. Some kids say she even looks like Mike Tyson and call her a butch behind her back. If I'm around her too much, who knows what else they'll say about me?

I also see The Mildred Rodriguez sitting at the other end of the yard. I call her The Mildred because she's the prettiest girl I've ever seen in my life. She's even prettier than girls on TV.

What I think?

I think God kept my share when beauty dust was being sprinkled.

Her boyfriend, Santos, is just as beautiful. Sometimes I stare at him so long I get dizzy. He's got slick jet-black hair, light brown eyes, permanently suntanned skin, a dimpled smile, and the whitest, straightest teeth.

I begin to picture Santos and me at a wedding. I have a smile that belongs in a toothpaste commercial. He's hypnotized by it, and I lead him to a beach nearby. We're strolling, the waves lick at our feet, and Santos looks into my big light green eyes and then—

Ike is coming my way!

I drop the rope and run inside the school. I head downstairs to the girls' bathroom in the basement and lock the door, wishing I had my mother's big dresser to put against it. I have to remember to write later in Malice: *Be stronger, run faster.*

I cover my eyes with my father's red handkerchief. I could be all right but it's too dark. I start feeling like I'm back in Haiti with those soldiers.

I uncover my eyes and back into a corner. I wait.

I swing open the door to my home: a two-bedroom apartment on Newkirk Avenue. Today was a good day. I got 100 on the English test and Ike didn't bust his way into the bathroom. It's Friday–T.G.I.N.–Thank God Ike's Nowhere.

I walk to the kitchen and find Grandmère Adda sitting at the table with a wooden mortar and pestle in her lap. My mother is at the sink seasoning meat.

"*Bonswa,* Grandmère. Hi, Maman," I greet them. "Want me to pound the spices?" I ask in Créole, a mix of French and other languages. I speak Créole with all the adults in my house. When they try to speak English, it's always broken and with an accent.

"Aaahhh, now you ask!" my grandmother says. "I'm done and my arm's about to fall off."

"You know what happened to me today?" I smile. "I got a hundred on my English test."

"Bravo. *Se bon,* keep going," Grandmère says. Then in English: "Kip goyin."

"Yes, that is good, very good," my mother says. "Tape your test on the front door."

"Aaahhh, all those years she and Serina spent with me I made sure they took their schoolwork seriously," says Grandmère. "I don't raise lazy children." She gets up and hands my mother the mortar with the crushed spices, then picks up a bowl of cut coconut and begins grating it. Oh, good, she's going to make coconut *tablèt.* She makes that and other sweets to sell by the train station. I see her there sometimes when I'm walking home from school. She's ready to run if she sees a police car because she doesn't have a permit to sell. In Haiti Grandmère owned and managed a grocery store, but here she can't even sell a bag of popcorn. She and my aunt Widza came to New York about eight months ago because things in Haiti were getting worse with all the killings and shootings. My uncle Perrin decided to stay and look after the house even though Grandmère didn't want him to. That uncle almost got us killed with his big mouth. We don't know where he is now.

"Is there a wedding, Maman?" I ask. There are huge buckets of meat on the kitchen counters. She worked at this cosmetics factory as long as I've been alive, but since it closed down, people have been hiring her to cook for their parties. They know she's good and can stretch a meal like that story in the Bible, the one about feeding thousands of people with one fish and a piece of bread.

"Clara Metro is marrying George Étienne," my mother answers. She rubs and rubs each piece of meat with lemon and sour oranges. The fat on her arms jiggles.

"Aaahhh!" says Grandmère, her arm also jiggling with every grate. "George Étienne is marrying that Clara Metro? He's just a boy! This will be Clara's third husband! Are they getting married in the church?"

"Of course," my mother says. "You know how Clara likes to show off. The priest won't marry them on the altar itself because Clara's been divorced. On or off the altar, she just wants to get married in a church because her last two marriages were at City Hall. Imagine you're forty-nine with five children, and marrying a man young enough to be your son. *Mézanmi!*"

"People who aren't afraid of *tripotay* will do anything," says Grandmère.

"It's good Clara Metro isn't afraid of gossip," I say.

Both Maman and Grandmère look at me.

"What do you mean it's good?" says Grandmère. "Is it good to have five children with five different men?"

"What does Mardi know?" Maman says, returning to her meat. "Children have three responsibilities: eat, sleep, and school."

I should have just kept my mouth shut. They always think I don't know anything. I know a lot of things. Did they ever get 100 on a test? Or jump double Dutch for six minutes straight, or know the best places to hide?

I go over to the stove and lift the lids of the pots and

pans. One pot has codfish in onions, the other boiled green plantains, and the other rice with red kidney beans the size of marbles. I move to the refrigerator and take out a bottle of West Indian fruit soda.

"Ey, put that back," Maman says. "You haven't eaten."

"You can take mine, Mardi." Grandmère points to a half-full glass on the table.

I suck my teeth.

"What?" Maman says. "What was that?"

"What?"

"Did you just *chipe* at me and your grandmother?"

"No." I didn't think she would hear me.

My mother stops and points at me. "Listen, Mardi. Watch your bones with me."

I put the soda back and keep myself from slamming the refrigerator door. I leave the kitchen and go past the front door, not stopping to put up my perfect English paper. It would have gone next to a picture of Serina and her beauty award certificate and below Aunt Widza's American dollar, the first money she made in this country. It was Aunt Widza's idea to tape our achievements on the front door "so each day when we leave the house, we know what we're capable of."

I go to the room I share with Serina, Grandmère, and Aunt Widza. I have about two hours to myself before Serina comes home. She works at the Bedford Avenue Salon de Beauté some weekdays and at a Haitian restaurant on weekends. Maman lets Serina work because she's eighteen, in her senior year at Clara Barton.

Aunt Widza works, too, a few afternoons a week at the

Amorez One-Stop Shopping Dominican Supermarket a few blocks away on Avenue D. Aunt Widza is my father's little sister, and she isn't really supposed to be working. She doesn't have her papers, for one, and . . . she's a little crazy. But Mr. Amorez, the owner, liked Aunt Widza the first day I took her in there. He wouldn't stop looking at her. Aunt Widza told him that if he liked looking at her that much, he should pay her. She started working there the next day.

We didn't want Aunt Widza working, but not so much because she didn't have her papers. My father had worked for Mr. Amorez for a while, back when Papa first came to New York and he didn't have all his papers, either. Mr. Amorez paid Papa under the table just like he's probably paying all the South American workers there now. All Aunt Widza does is mop floors and take care of fruits and vegetables, but the problem is, Aunt Widza is unpredictable. A few months ago when she was off her medication, she went to the Brooklyn Botanic Garden. All the men she met there followed her home that day. It wasn't only because they thought she was pretty. Aunt Widza had made each of them a promise, which she wouldn't tell us even when Papa threatened to call the police on the men ringing our doorbell.

I don't want Aunt Widza at the supermarket for a different reason. Mr. Amorez is Santos's father.

I first saw Santos at the grand opening of the new and bigger Amorez Supermarket. Everything was on sale. When my mother went to buy meat, I waited for her in the next aisle over. I didn't want to stand next to her because they had whole roasted pigs tied and hanging by sticks in the meat section, and I thought I saw one of the pigs wink at me.

"Kapone!" my mother teased me. "You chicken." The men behind the counter laughed with her.

I looked at my reflection on a pole covered in shiny aluminum. I had on these tight high-water royal blue polyester pants and a pink sweater that was four sizes too big. Then something bumped into me. When I turned around I saw this beautiful . . . thing standing in front of me with a shopping cart.

It was Santos.

"What?" he asked.

"Huh?" I said.

"You not gonna move?"

"Huh?"

"I said excuse me!"

"Huh?"

"Mardi!" my mother yelled at me from across the next aisle. "Stop-eh stand like that, like eh big dommy, and move for deh boy." Finally I understood and stepped aside. As Santos walked close past me, I could smell the Old Spice soap on his neck and I thought of boats and ships, sunshine and water. Seeing him made me want to kiss my mother and those men in the meat section who had laughed at me earlier.

In the bedroom I look at my English test and the big red mark at the top of it: the number one followed by two smiling zeroes. What a beautiful number. I take out Malice and fill a page with those three numbers.

I spray my English test with perfume and slide it under my pillow.

I start thinking of Santos. I don't want to watch TV even though I'm allowed to on Fridays and weekends. I don't feel like reading or looking over my rock collection. I don't even want to work on one of my thousand-piece puzzles stacked up neatly in the closet.

No, I'm thinking about Santos and I need to dance!

I close the bedroom door and turn on Serina's radio. I look in the mirror and I don't see the girl with the flat nose, wide lips, and pepper dots on her face. I don't see the girl who has *dèyè tèt grenn,* who can never grow good, strong, thick hair at the back of her head. I pretend the whole world is watching me dance.

"Shake it, *Mar*-cia!"

"Move it, *Mar*-garet!"

"Groove it, *Mar*-go!"

The world wants to know why I am so talented and beautiful.

Listen to my music:

I pretend the poster on our wall of Reggie Miller dunking a basketball comes alive. After the ball goes in, Reggie stops and looks at me, astonished. He calls over Michael Jordan, who's shooting a ball in another poster nearby. Michael calls Jean-Claude Van Damme, and then Santos. Yes, Santos is in the picture, too. It's a good fantasy, my fantasy.

I sing my favorite song and theirs, "I Will Always Love

You." My voice makes them forget about everything else. Reggie has tears in his eyes, and Santos, beautiful Santos, steps out of the picture and into my room, which is now a grand ballroom. He's wearing a white tuxedo and I am in a skintight red gown with big red feathers at the shoulder. And my breasts are much larger than they are now. Santos takes my hand and whispers something in Spanish.

"Yo he esperado para este momento."

He moves in closer to me . . . smiling . . .

I close . . .

my eyes . . .

and then . . .

he . . .

he—

A sound comes from the closet. Santos, Reggie, Michael, and Jean-Claude disappear. The closet door creaks open. My aunt Widza's smile is as big as the moon. She has on a bright red hat with a white feather tucked at the side. She's wearing my father's huge winter coat and sandals with socks. I would laugh at her but I'm too surprised and angry. I hate being interrupted. She starts clapping.

"I love you, Mardi. I did not let him kiss me. Now take me home."

"What?" I grab her hand and take her to the kitchen.

"Oh, no," says Grandmère. "It's starting again."

I leave them and go back to the room.

Even in Haiti Aunt Widza was a little off. She climbed trees to talk to the birds and fruit, and sometimes she'd wake everyone up in the middle of the night so we could watch her dance in the backyard. She called it her liberation dance. Grandmère had to give her medication to calm her down. But there was nothing Grandmère could do when Aunt Widza didn't speak for days and stayed in a corner like a scared rabbit. When she got here, Maman and Papa took her to see a doctor, and the doctor said she wasn't a dangerous person, just someone who sometimes had a different way of doing things, and that medication would help balance her moods.

Aunt Widza can read and write and isn't stupid, not at all. Sometimes I see her looking through Serina's textbooks and reading the dictionary in French and English. She has notebooks of songs she's written. She knows a little something about everything. But lately her thing is to say "I love you." I was walking with her last week on Nostrand Avenue when she suddenly puckered her lips and started blowing kisses at every strange man walking by.

Smack! "I love you, baby."

At first it was funny to see how shocked the men were. They didn't know what to say. I liked that Aunt Widza didn't care, but then, that was the problem, too. She didn't even notice the men behind us grabbing their crotches and laughing, following us like bees that had spotted honey. I had to pull her to walk faster, then run. They stopped following, but I held on to Aunt Widza and kept running.

A week later we get the news.

I'm watching *The Sound of Music* for the twelfth time with Aunt Widza, and each time is like her first. She's just taken a bath and I can smell her shampoo and the lavender oil she uses on her body. She used to have her permed hair way past her shoulders, but when she moved in with us she had cut it all off and let it grow natural, like black cotton.

"Matant," I whisper. "Do you remember that jump-rope song we used to sing . . . ?"

She slowly shakes her head. All she knows right now is *The Sound of Music,* the part where the oldest daughter is crying because her father won't let her see some boy.

I listen to my mother and grandmother having their supper of *bouyon* in the kitchen:

Slurp. Smack. Slurp. Smack.

The stew must be good tonight.

"I love this movie," Aunt Widza says. She finally looks up at me. "Oh, Mardi, *ti anj mwen,* my little angel. You were asking your aunt about a song, right?"

"Forget it," I tell her. That's when my father bursts through the front door, waving a piece of paper in his hand.

"We got a letter!" he shouts. "We got a letter about Perrin!"

My mother and grandmother rush out of the kitchen. Aunt Widza jumps out of her seat.

"Kisa?" asks Grandmère. "Is he . . . alive?"

"Yes," my father says with the letter in his hand. "Perrin is alive!"

"Aaahhh, Saint Joseph!" Grandmère Adda cries, clapping her hands. "Saint Joseph!"

"He's been in the camps at Guantánamo Bay, Cuba, as we suspected," Papa continues. "The Americans are granting him political asylum and he'll be here in a few weeks!"

They jump for joy. I get up and stop *The Sound of Music. Monnonk.* My uncle Perrin. He's the real reason why we all had to leave Haiti so suddenly. He's the reason Serina and I had to hide out in the woods and cornfields with little food and water.

Before I left Port-au-Prince, there was a coup d'état. Some people tried to kill the president of Haiti and everyone who supported him. But my uncle Perrin and his friends played hero and went on the radio, gave out flyers, and wrote graffiti against the coup. They did this even though people were hiding away or falling dead like drops in a rainstorm.

I saw bodies lying in our street when I looked out our window. One day I counted three. We heard stories of people we knew being tortured and killed in the worst ways. We heard screams coming from the house across the street, screams that didn't stop for days. Grandmère was so afraid. When she wasn't talking directly to a person, she was saying a prayer, any prayer that came to mind. Grandmère's grocery store was in another part of the city and so she had to keep it closed. No one left the house except a servant who went out during the day to buy food. Grandmère had covered all the windows and doors with black sheets, shutting out any sunlight, as if being in the dark and staying quiet would make it all stop. She had Serina and me with her everywhere she went.

Then they killed my cousin Philippe and dumped his body in front of our house. They called out Uncle Perrin's name when they drove away. I didn't eat for two days afterward. Philippe was only fifteen and slow in the head. I had liked him. He gave me piggyback rides to school and played tea party with me when my sister wouldn't. Right after Philippe died, Maman and Papa sent for Serina and me. I was supposed to leave Haiti for New York when I was sixteen, but I left when I was twelve.

A year after Serina and I left, things still hadn't gotten any better, so Grandmère and Aunt Widza also left the country. Someone had set fire to Grandmère's store and she was attacked on the street. They'd knocked out a few of her teeth and promised to kill her, too. They were still looking for Uncle Perrin, who was in and out of hiding. Grandmère didn't want to leave him behind, but he begged her and Aunt Widza to leave. It's been almost a year since we heard from Uncle Perrin. Every week my father goes to the Haitian embassy to see if his name turns up on any list.

I walk past my father and the letter, trying not to hear all the questions from my mother, grandmother, and aunt. I would go to the bedroom but Serina is there babbling on the phone. So I go to the bathroom and I lean against the door. I say all the curse words I know in English, then translate them into Créole.

Uncle Perrin is coming!

Things had been fine with me in Haiti. Yes, I didn't like it when I first got there; I was only four and didn't know if I'd see my mother and father again. But I got used to the place. Every few months they came to visit and I realized I hadn't lost them. Port-au-Prince was a good place to be. It was summer all year long, and Serina and I went to a good Catholic school with the money Maman and Papa sent to Grandmère.

Grandmère's big house had three floors of balconies full of plants. She had dogs and cats and a parakeet in her backyard. My grandfather had built the house before my father was born, but it always smelled like it had just been built. Back then the houses were mostly made of wood, but my grandfather knew he wanted to build something his grandchildren could use. He made his house out of thick cement and painted it the same color as the sky because he believed the sky was forever. There were at least eight bedrooms and four separate rooms outside for servants. I lived with cousins, aunts, uncles, and friends who became family, but the house was never crowded.

It was a Sunday morning the day we left Port-au-Prince. I'm sure it was Sunday because the church bells were ringing. Serina and I and a few neighbors who were also leaving came together for a small mass and prayer at the pastor's house next door to my grandmother's. Grandmère had let me wear my Easter dress, one of my favorites; it was yellow and ruffled at the collar. She gave me back a pink Barbie purse she had taken away from me months before, for what I can't remember.

After the pastor said the prayers, we all got into an old army truck and headed for the airport. But right before we got there, men started shooting at us. Maybe they thought Uncle Perrin was in the truck. The truck made a turn and half an hour later we were deep in La Pleine, the countryside.

I don't want to remember too much, but these things are like sleeping hiccups in my head. I know the truck got two flat tires from the bullets. Everyone got out running and screaming. I ran with my pink Barbie purse close to my chest. Serina and I stayed together with some people from the truck. Someone had a portable radio and we heard that the airport was closed. We had to spend two days hiding in the woods and cornfields. One morning I went to look for water and I got lost. The cornstalks were tall and yellow like my dress. . . . When I got back, Serina was crying because she didn't know where I was. Soon after, another truck full of people rescued us and took us to the airport.

We flew straight to New York. When we were waiting for Maman and Papa to come pick us up at Kennedy Airport, I couldn't find my pink Barbie purse.

"Where did you leave it?" Serina asked.

"I don't remember," I said, and started crying.

"Oh, stop that," she said. "We're in the country that makes Barbies. You'll find your purse in all colors here."

When I didn't stop crying, Serina went to buy me some bubble gum, the kind I liked that had the juicy syrup in the middle. I took the whole pack from her and ran to the bathroom. I went inside a stall, unwrapped all the pieces. I stuffed each one in my mouth. I chewed so fast I almost bit off my tongue.

The bathroom window is open. I smell the night breeze but I feel hot and sticky, like I've been running through cornfields with the sun on my back. Without taking off my clothes, I get into the shower. I turn on the cold water, letting it hit my forehead. It feels like winter when I'm not wearing a hat. I undo my cornrow braids and wash my hair even though it isn't dirty. I massage my scalp the way Aunt Widza used to when I was little. Sometimes I'd let her wash my hair under the *cha cha* tree in Grandmère's backyard. I'd fall asleep with soap in my hair, and when I would wake up, I'd be on a bed with my hair braided, smelling like sweet mango.

I must have visited my father's yard at least a dozen times waiting for Uncle Perrin to come. On weekdays my father is a handyman at this big law office in Manhattan, and on some nights he drives his *taptap* van, picking up passengers for one-dollar rides. On weekends Papa is the part-time manager at a reusable-things yard he half owns on Utica Avenue. It's really a junkyard, but I hate to say the word "junk." When I was first learning English, I had one of Serina's friends, Rosslyn, as a tutor. Rosslyn used to say: "Mardi, what's all this junk you're writing? What's all this junk you're reading?" Rosslyn loved "junk," but I didn't and gave it a better name.

One day after school I go there and search the yard for things to sell to Pierre LeBalle. She loves to collect dolls and small toys. She has a closet full of them. Pierre would buy the moon from me, and if I could, I'd sell it to her in slices.

I find an alarm clock radio with some knobs missing and think about selling it to Serina since she's always waking up late. Then I remember the blow-dryer I sold her for five dollars. I had to give the money back because she got an electric shock when she plugged it in.

After shopping for Pierre I sit with my notebook, Malice, on a chair in the middle of the yard. The yard is not a smelly dump. It just has piles of things people don't want anymore or can't fix. I sit in the middle of all these things and feel like I understand them. I open Malice and write my uncle's name twenty times. Some names I underline twice, others I cross out, and the rest I question. While I'm doing this, my father comes up to me and places his hand on my head.

"What are you doing here again? I thought you only came on Saturdays."

I don't answer. He takes his hand away and slips it in his pocket.

"Your sister hates coming here. The garbage bothers her. What a little princess."

I still don't say anything, wishing he'd put his warm hand back on my head.

"Your mother's another one. If it's not in the Macy's catalog, it's no good, and yet she lives for when things go on sale. You know the gems I've found in this place?" He runs his hand over his silver-and-black hair. He's fifteen years older than my mother, but if he'd dye his hair black, he'd look ten years younger than her.

An old, rattling truck pulls up at the Haitian bakery across the street.

"Ey," Papa says. "Are you hungry?"

"No."

"Why are you never hungry? You have to eat so your body will stay solid against any sickness you get."

"Okay, I want a coconut *tablèt* and *bonbon lanmidon*."

"Just sweets? You can have your grandmother make that for you. You need salt in your body, too. Your mother was saying this morning she might make conch in vegetable sauce for the Sunday meal. She knows you like that."

"Really? She hasn't made that in a long time."

"It's an expensive dish. But her food business is going well." He picks up something from the ground. "I was looking for a screw this size."

"Papa?"

"Yes?"

"Are you happy Uncle Perrin is coming?"

"What kind of question is that? He's my little brother, of course I'm happy. Aren't you? When I used to visit you and your sister in Haiti, sometimes I'd think you two didn't know I was your father, the way you clung to Perrin. You of all people should be jumping for joy, right? Mardi?"

"Can I get a beef pattie then?"

"Mardi, don't you want to be with your uncle Perrin?"

I shrug. "Yes."

"That's what I thought." He gives me some money. "Buy some patties for the house, too."

Although Isaac Washington Carver has gotten left back twice and is the oldest student at Taliaferro, I do believe he has a goal: making sure I am killed or seriously injured. As I go down the steps to the lunchroom, Ike is waiting for me halfway there. I keep my head down and slow my breathing. I should be used to this by now.

Ike trips me and I hit my face against the banister and cut my bottom lip open. The whole cafeteria is laughing. When Mrs. Orlando comes running to me, Ike pretends he's helping me up. He holds out his hand but I'm afraid to take it.

"Are you okay, Mardi?" asks Mrs. Orlando.

I nod and get up on my own.

"Isaac, get back to your class or wherever it is you're supposed to be," Mrs. Orlando tells him. When Ike doesn't move, she puts her hands on her apple-shaped hips and glares at him.

"Yeah, right, Miami—I mean, Mrs. Orlando," Ike says. He throws my book bag at me. "Be careful." He winks.

A few minutes later I'm sitting alone on the edge of a bench, swallowing the blood on my lips. Tears drip into my tomato soup. I'm pinching my arm real hard. The pain there hurts more than anything else. I feel better even though my arm is sore. The soreness will go away in a little while and take some of Ike with it.

Mrs. Orlando comes to sit next to me.

"Are you all right, Mardi?" she asks, touching my arm. I cringe and pull away.

"Is your arm all right?"

I nod and sniff.

"Oh, don't cry," she says. "Listen, Isaac's a big bully. I'm sure inside he's just a scared little boy." She reaches to pat my hand but I pull away from her a little too quick. Her hand hangs in the air for a few seconds, and then she places it gently on the table. That's too bad because I do like Mrs. Orlando. After all, she gave me Malice. I have to remember to write something nice about her. Maybe write a special prayer so her husband will return. Everyone keeps saying he ran off with the woman who cuts his hair.

"Are you writing in your journal?" she asks.

"I was just thinking about him right now," I answer.

"Him?"

"My journal is a boy."

"That's so interesting. I'm glad you're keeping up and going beyond. Two years ago you didn't even speak English. But you went to tutoring every day and read and reread all your textbooks. You've worked hard and now you're one of the best students in the school. Well-deserved praise, and I'm not just saying that because you fell down the stairs." She laughs a little.

"If Ike had pushed me, Mrs. Orlando, would you send him to the principal?"

"You could send Ike to heaven and he'd still come back the same." Mrs. Orlando and a lot of the other teachers don't like Ike much. Ike yells at the teachers, and spits at them, and once he said he was going to shoot one of them for not letting him come to class late.

"You, on the other hand, Mardi," Mrs. Orlando continues, "you're a good kid. Don't forget that. I know I'm not wasting my time with you. Keep safe." She gets up, yelling after someone who isn't recycling his milk cartons.

Keep safe, she says? What a challenge. What I should

have told Mrs. Orlando is that the first day I met Ike, I came home crying. He had me in a corner in the schoolyard, calling me all kinds of nasty names. I'd only been in the country a few weeks and was so scared of everything. So when I came home crying, I told everyone that some kids were making fun of the cornrows in my hair. Serina wanted to give me a perm but my mother said no. She said I had to be a rock and not hand people my feelings so easily. My father told me not to pay any attention to these kids. He said when all their chemically treated hair fell out, I'd be the only one standing proud with virgin hair. I got mad at all of them: Maman, Papa, and Serina. I got mad because they couldn't read my mind or see through my lies.

One day I came home with both my knees cut. Even though Ike had tripped me, I told everyone I fell. The fall bruised my right knee but I took care of my left. Whatever Ike gave me, I matched it. That first year I started Taliaferro, I was coming home with bruises from Ike and from me. Everyone thought I was clumsy. I let them believe what I let them see.

Since school began this year, Ike hasn't touched me much. I run faster now, but I can still hear what he says to me. I don't know what it is about me that makes Ike hate me so much. He picks on a lot of other people at school, but I feel like he saves his most wicked tricks for me. At first I thought it was because I was Haitian. He always called me "Haitian" this and "island" that. There are lots of other Haitian kids at Taliaferro I could hang out with, but they're too "American" to have anything to do with me.

They wear clothes that would fit a hippo and they forget how to speak Créole. Last year when I came in with my mother's *pen patat* for the Christmas class party, they said the sweet potato pie looked like something from the toilet bowl.

Please! As if they've never eaten the stuff!

And when I first started school, they were the first ones to accuse me of having Haitian Body Odor. Somehow they knew how to get rid of theirs.

I take Malice out of my book bag. I write: *Maybe teasing me somehow proves how American they are—or how Haitian I am.*

I'm easy to spot with my polyester dresses while everyone else in school wears jeans and sneakers. I still have my hair in cornrows and wear baby barrettes while every girl in school either has a perm or braided extensions. Serina badly wants to perm my hair because she's the one who has to do my hair every Sunday night.

"Your hair is like Brillo," she said to me once as she worked. "My fingernails are at your mercy."

"All you have to do is braid it," I told her, "not wear it. Be happy you're not me."

She stopped and looked at me in the mirror. "What do you mean by that?"

"Nothing."

I look around the cafeteria. Everyone is having a good time eating.

What I think?

I think maybe there's something in the food that makes these people happy at lunchtime.

The Mildred Rodriguez is surrounded, as usual, by all the other popular kids in the school, none as pretty as her. She's got long thick black hair that comes down to her waist and hazel eyes like Santos.

So Santos likes pretty girls? What boy doesn't? Me standing next to Mildred is like a city pigeon standing next to a swan that just flew in from heaven. The only words she's ever said to me are "Hey, you little FOB"—meaning Fresh Off the Boat, a refugee. That was when I first started school here and it was all over the news that Haitians were taking boats like crazy out of Haiti, taking boats going wherever. I don't think FOB fits me because I came here by plane, not boat. And when I got off the plane I wasn't fresh, either.

Pierre LeBalle waves at me from another corner of the cafeteria. That boy is sitting next to her, her cousin or something, the one I saw her playing basketball with in the courtyard. What's his name again? Anyway, I wave back, praying she and her doofy friends don't come over. If I look like I just stepped off the boat, Pierre and her friends look like they've never gotten off, and she's been here since she was four. Pierre and I used to be good friends, mostly because we lived in the same building and our fathers were friends. I used to watch Saturday-morning cartoons at her house because she had a TV in her room.

When I first came to Brooklyn, she was the one who showed me around the neighborhood, told me the best places to buy good cheap candy. She showed me shortcuts from home to anywhere and told me the streets and alleys to stay away from, places where bums peed and where people sold and smoked crack.

I guess she would have become my best friend except she was always asking me about Haiti.

What's it like now?

Is it still sunny?

Did I go to the beaches a lot?

Pierre hadn't been there in a long time. I was trying to get rid of Haiti in my mind and she kept wanting to go there, sucking my memory like hard candy.

I shut Malice and open the book I'm reading: *Roll of Thunder, Hear My Cry.* Jilline's grandfather saved it especially for me to read. Mr. Hunter is a retired policeman and works at the Flatbush public library.

I met Mr. Hunter before I knew he was Jilline's grandfather. I was going over to the library's information desk one day when I saw this girl with buck teeth, freckles, and long curly red braids spinning around in his chair. I recognized her from school.

"You must be the reading princess," she said when I reached the desk.

I didn't understand.

"My grandfather says there's this girl who comes into the library, who goes to my school, who's in the same grade I'm in, and who's reading all the books here. It must be you. Your head's in a book every time I see you."

I was surprised she noticed me. "Mr. Hunter is your grandfather?"

"Yep."

Wow, I thought. I'm connected. Jilline hung around The Mildred Rodriguez sometimes but wasn't stuck-up. She smiled at me a few times and once even helped me pick up my books when Ike tripped me.

"You sure do like books," she said, still spinning from side to side. I was getting dizzy watching her.

"Yes," I said. "*Dey* help me." She heard my accent.

"Where're you from?" she asked.

"Newkirk Avenue."

"No, I mean you Haitian?"

"Y-yes."

"Oh." She looked at me for a moment, no expression on her face. When she figured I wasn't going to say anything more, she continued, "My last boyfriend was Haitian. I met him at the West Indian Day parade."

I had to laugh because when she smiled she looked like Bugs Bunny. We became friends right after that.

Later in science class, Jilline asks me:

"Do you know who Santos Amorez is going solo with?" We are partners, about to dissect a frog. I stare at the dead frog lying belly-up on the table in front of us. Jilline has her sharp scissors and is preparing to cut it open when I push her hand away.

"We should say a prayer."

Jilline rolls her eyes and begins on the frog. I feel like she's cutting my own stomach. I feel the cold edge of the scissors tracing a line from between my legs up to my chin.

"Santos is going solo with Mildred Rodriguez, who else?" she tells me, as if I couldn't guess. "You know he's been going on and off with her now for months. Now Santos wants her to be the only one."

"Oh." Now it's official. But I'm not going to stop thinking of Santos.

Even if I were the one Santos wanted, I wouldn't know how to be someone's girlfriend. Maman and Papa say a girl thinking about boyfriends at fourteen years old will be a mother by fifteen.

I shrug. "The Mildred—I mean, that girl is very pretty."

"She's a dog!" Jilline says. "You take away the long hair, hazel eyes, long eyelashes, the perfect mouth and set of teeth, she'd be a dog! *Wuf! Wuf!*"

I laugh. "I can't change who I like—I mean, who Santos likes," I say.

"Well, if you would stop wearing that gray uniform every day, maybe Santos might notice you."

I stop laughing.

"What? What did I say?" Jilline asks, noticing my mood change.

I shake my head and bite my lip hard.

"You gotta tell me if I said something wrong."

"No *ting*—I mean, no *thing*."

"Fine, whatever," she says, focusing her attention back on the frog. "My granddaddy says people don't get what they want by keeping their mouths shut, you know."

On my way home I think about what Jilline said about me wearing the same clothes almost every day. . . .

Oh, what does she know? She's rich. Her grandfather

has lots of money and owns a brownstone. Mr. Hunter only works at the library because he wants to.

When I look up, I find myself in front of the Amorez Supermarket. This is my cathedral. Then, through the glass windows I catch a glimpse of Aunt Widza laughing with a shopper. I spin around and bump into . . . Santos, my other cathedral.

The three-ring binder I'm carrying falls to the ground. Santos picks it up.

"Hey." He smiles as if I've just said something funny. He hands me my binder, but when he moves to walk around me, my feet do something amazing: they step to the side and block his way. Santos and I are both surprised.

"See you," he says, and walks around me again into his father's store.

Oh, the world is wonderful! I walk home thinking about Santos and me in the grand ballroom again. When I enter the lobby of my building, I see Pierre's cousin getting the mail.

"Hi, Mardi," he says.

"Hi," I answer. "What's your name again?"

"Patrick Novembre."

"Oh. You're Pierre's cousin, right?"

"Yeah, my mother and her father are brother and sister. Me and my mother just moved here from Boston. We're living with Pierre and her father."

"Is the apartment crowded now?"

"Not really. They have an extra bedroom."

"You're not in any of my classes."

"Yeah, I'm in eighth grade." He holds up a bag of

coconut *tablèt*. "I got these today by the train station from your grandmother. They're real good. My mother likes them, too." He takes a bite and runs up the stairs. As I'm about to head up myself, I hear Serina calling me.

"*Biskwit! Biskwit!* Wait for me!" I turn around and see her at the door trying to find her keys. She calls me biscuit because when I was young, I only wanted to eat lemon cookies and soda crackers.

"Why are you home so early?" I open the door for her.

"I have a chemistry test tomorrow. I need to study." She has on bright red lipstick with black eyeliner outlining the shape of her full lips. She lets loose her ponytail and shakes her hair all over her face. Then she gives me her famous dimpled smile. Everybody looks at Serina when she walks down the street. She isn't skinny and she isn't fat. She's just right. And Serina doesn't need to wear much makeup, either—all she needs to do is show some teeth.

We start the walk up the three flights of stairs to our apartment. When we get to the second floor, she grabs my book bag, stopping me.

"Listen, Biskwit," she says, "I need you to help me write something. I just got my college applications from school today and I need you to write my essay."

"Why should I?"

"Because I'm your sister and I'm older than you."

I begin climbing the last flight of stairs, and this time she grabs the arm I fell on when Ike tripped me on the stairs. I flinch.

"What's wrong with your arm?" she asks.

"I slept on it all last night."

"Oh. You shouldn't do that. Anyway, I'll pay you if you write my essay."

"I'll think about it."

"Have Grandmère rub your arm tonight. Here, give me your bag. You're lucky you have such a nice big sister."

"Oh, please." I hand her my heavy book bag even though we only have half a flight of stairs left to reach home.

I'm dreaming in shades of violet and black again. I haven't had those dreams in a long time. I got rid of them by sleeping with rocks in my bed. The rocks make me uncomfortable and I can't sleep well. If I can't sleep well, my dreams are choppy and forgettable.

Last night, thanks to Uncle Perrin, the soldiers came again. Two are chasing me through the cornfields. The sky is violet, the corn is blue, and the ground is black. The soldiers are moving closer. I can even smell their sweat. I'm running in place. When they reach me, they turn into three-legged barking dogs. Their fur is black but their eyes are blue. I suddenly see I'm in quicksand and I wonder why there's quicksand in cornfields. I'm sinking but I can't stay still. The dogs want to bite my head off because I'm alone and a girl. Just as my face goes under—

I wake up in Brooklyn.

I try to take a deep breath but my nose is bleeding. I wipe the blood away with the back of my hand. The door is closed and the heater is shishing out steam. I slide down from the top bunk. Serina is snoring in the bottom bunk, dreaming of better things, I'm sure. Some Sleeping Beauty; Sleeping Beauty never snored like Serina.

I go to the window and open it wide. If I had enough guts, I'd scream and wake up all of Brooklyn. The cold air and the steam's hot breath meet on my skin, and for a moment I feel like I'm flying, melting in a tingle.

Soon enough I get cold. I push the window down, leaving it open a crack. I pull the shades halfway up so the light that's coming from the moon can help me see in the dark. I stand in the middle of the room, dizzy, as if I've just stopped spinning.

I slowly open the closet door. I run my hand over the puzzle boxes neatly stacked on the side shelf.

Maybe I should work on one?

No. I don't feel like that tonight. Instead, I search for my rocks. I find their small gray velvet bag and stick my hand in, feeling the smooth, cool pebbles and rough rocks I got from Grandmère Adda's backyard right before I left. I sprinkle some on my bed, but I don't want to sleep there anymore tonight. I take my blanket and pillow and go across the room to Grandmère and Aunt Widza. I curl up between them on the sofa bed. I match my breathing with theirs until I fall asleep.

In the morning I wake up with Grandmère Adda's hand on my face. She's lying on her stomach with one arm dangling off the side.

Aunt Widza hums like a refrigerator. She has a silly smile on her face, as if someone's whispering a secret joke to her, tickling her with a feather from the inside.

A question suddenly comes to my mind as my father is driving us all to Kennedy Airport to pick up Uncle Perrin.

"Where's he going to sleep?" I ask.

There's silence. I guess no one else had thought about it, either.

"He'll sleep on the sofa in the living room," Papa says.

"Aaahhh! Trust me, that sofa is very uncomfortable," says Grandmère. "It almost broke my back."

"Then we'll buy another sofa bed," my mother says.

"But what about his luggage, his things?" I ask. "Where are we going to put them?"

"Mardi, stop asking questions," snaps Maman. "Perrin was at a refugee camp. He's not coming here with suitcases of Gucci clothes."

"Don't worry," says Serina, sitting next to me. "You won't have to give up your precious little bed." She leans her head back, listening to her Walkman. I reach over for the headphones and she pushes my hand away.

"I want to listen."

"Stop," she says. "You do this every time we're in the car."

I whisper in her ear, "College essay? College essay?" She squints at me and drops the Walkman in my lap.

At the airport we have no problem finding Uncle

Perrin. He's wearing a bright orange jacket and blue-brown checked bell-bottom pants. In one hand he has a broken guitar, and in the other, a small boy carrying a yellow plastic umbrella. My uncle is grinning, but the boy is frowning at us.

Everyone rushes to embrace Uncle Perrin. Everyone except me.

"Aaahhh! Here's my boy! Here's my son!" my grandmother shouts.

Aunt Widza picks up the boy, kisses him, then swings him around. Then she asks him, "Who are you?"

"Pélé," he says seriously. "Perrin is my father."

"I met Pélé in the refugee camp at Guantánamo Bay," Uncle Perrin says. Then, really low, he says, "He doesn't have a mother or father."

For a moment we stand looking at Pélé, who stares fiercely back at us.

"Why didn't you just give him to immigration?" I ask. We don't need two extra people in our apartment.

"Shut your mouth, Mardi," my mother warns.

"Pélé doesn't have anyone right now," Uncle Perrin continues. "His mother saved my life in the camp. I got sick and she took care of me. She caught pneumonia and–"

"Aaahhh! You don't have to explain yourself to anyone!" Grandmère tells him. "You're here with your family and no harm can come to you now! Oh, Perrin!" She hugs him again.

"Mardi," Perrin says, "aren't you going to say hello to your favorite uncle?"

By hello he means a kiss on the cheek. I hold out my hand to him. Everyone laughs.

"Look at this little American!" Uncle Perrin grabs my arm, but Pélé separates us before he can hug me.

"*Pa touche!* Don't touch my father!" he says. He only speaks Créole.

"Oh, how sweet," says Serina.

"He's my little guardian," Uncle Perrin says.

How lucky for you, I say to myself. Under my breath I ask, "Where the hell are you going to sleep?" My mother hears me and makes a move to grab me but I back away in time.

On our way to the parking lot everyone's walking ahead of me. Uncle Perrin is a hero returning home. Quick, raise the flags! Throw confetti! I'm the only one who notices him limping a little and holding his side. He's hurt, maybe?

Good.

Driving back to Brooklyn, Uncle Perrin sits in the passenger seat, where my mother was. I'm in the middle row between Aunt Widza and Grandmère Adda. Pélé is sitting on Aunt Widza's lap. My mother and Serina are in the back row with Uncle Perrin's camouflage duffel bag stamped PROPERTY OF U.S. COAST GUARD.

I have Serina's Walkman. I see everyone's mouth moving fast, probably asking my uncle how he and Pélé didn't get killed in Haiti and how they lived at the refugee camps at Guantánamo Bay. Who cares? I got out alive.

I'm about to switch the radio station when Pélé yanks the headphones from my ears.

"Let me hear it!" he says, as if the Walkman is his.

"Give that back!" I yell at him, grabbing back one end of the headphones. They stretch like a rubber band.

Pélé starts crying. "I want it! Give it! I want it!" Then he bites my hand.

"Ow!" I smack him on his head and he starts to cry real hard.

"What's wrong with Pélé?" my father asks.

"It's Mardi," my mother says, pinching and digging her nails behind my neck. "She's had that thing glued to her ears ever since we got in the car, and when this poor boy wants to listen to it, she won't let him. I'm the one who bought that Walkman. Give it to him, right now!"

I throw the Walkman at Pélé and it hits the window. Luckily, it doesn't break. Before anyone can say anything I quickly say, "Sorry."

"Look at Mardi," my mother says, "throwing things now. Maybe I'm not seeing right."

"Aaahh! *Se la raj!*" Grandmère says. "Kids in this country are in a rage. Watch TV, you'll know what I mean."

"Rage is good," Aunt Widza whispers, but no one but me hears her.

"Mardi is a good girl, huh, Biskwit?" Uncle Perrin says. When I don't answer, he continues, "Pélé gets into trouble, too. Sometimes he even gets me angry. There was this one time when we were in the camps . . ." And my uncle goes on telling stories about the adventures of little Pélé and the yellow umbrella.

"Keep the Walkman," Aunt Widza whispers to Pélé at

one point. She kisses him and holds him close to her. "You are safe here. Your family will protect you."

I pinch my thighs and grit my teeth until my head hurts. Traitor, I want to yell at her, you've never said that to me.

Tonight our apartment is festive. My father is playing
his favorite Nemours Jean-Baptiste record at full blast, as if
the house is cruising down Eastern Parkway. Pierre and
her father and Patrick and his mother are here, too. Pierre
wanted to come into my room, but I pretended I was
asleep. Now I'm here by myself.

I outline a circle on the back of my hand with one of
my mother's stainless steel knives. I press down too hard
and break my skin. I bite the cut. It doesn't hurt much.

When I go to the bathroom to get a Band-Aid, I smell
the Jane Barboncourt five-star rum in the air. They're all in
the kitchen. Mr. LeBalle and my father are smoking Cuban
cigars. Patrick and his mother sit quietly by the window.
His mother is so small and looks so timid.

Grandmère is pouring *du ris au lait* in bowls for everyone. Uncle Perrin loves *du ris au lait* and so do I. I love the

way Grandmère Adda makes hot rice pudding with vanilla and cinnamon sticks and brown sugar. She's serving it with fresh bread from the Haitian bakery and this really good butter we get from Montreal.

There are comforters and blankets on the living room floor for Uncle Perrin. Pélé, that little punk, is already asleep on the sofa. The Walkman is strapped to his head. I sit on the edge of the sofa and listen to the voices in the kitchen:

Grandmère: "Aaahhh, Perrin! I should hope now you'll abandon your active revolutionary days!"

Uncle Perrin: "Never. I'm going to die on my feet."

Grandmère: "You're so hardheaded!"

Aunt Widza: "No, he's got a soft head. That is why he cares so much about what happens to other people."

Grandmère: "Aaahhh! I don't know when this crisis will be over so Widza and I can return home."

Pierre: "Where did you get the guitar?"

Serina: "Yes, can you play?"

Uncle Perrin: "I made friends with a soldier in the camps. He taught me how to play, and when I was leaving, he gave me the guitar. This big lady on the plane sat on it by accident and it broke."

Pélé moves in his sleep. At first I think he's just changing positions, but he takes the covers and wraps them around himself, tucking his body tightly into the sofa. He starts sniffing and cooing like a bird. I walk around to him. His small face is sweating and trembling. What's the matter with him? Did he bring some memories over with him, too? I touch his wet face. This calms him down.

Papa: "Well, Perrin, you're in a different country now."

Mr. LeBalle: "You need a job and a social security number, in that order."

Uncle Perrin: "I need to get in touch with a few friends of mine. They'll help me get settled."

Grandmère: "Don't go mixing with people who will get you into trouble."

Uncle Perrin: "No, Maman, these all are people you know, people I went to school with. Do you remember . . ."

I'm about to remove my hand when Pélé suddenly opens his eyes and sits up.

"Maman?" he asks me, feeling the bedsheets around him.

"Oui?" I answer. Sure. I could be his mother for a minute.

"What did you do with my mother?"

I can't fool him. He backs away.

"Shhh. Don't be afraid," I whisper to him. "I won't hurt you." But Pélé swings his arm, his fist landing on my face. He jumps off the sofa and runs into the kitchen with his pillow.

"Hey! *Ti Pélé!*" The happiness in their voices blows away the tiny moment of pity I had for him. I sit down, holding my face.

Maman: "Poor thing. Why are his pajamas so wet?"

Aunt Widza: "Maybe he was swimming in his sleep."

Grandmère: "Come here, sweetheart. I hope it's not a fever."

Papa: "Serina, go change his clothes. Give him one of Mardi's old T-shirts or something to wear."

Uncle Perrin: "He won't let you touch him right now. I

know what to do. He just wants to be around people. He doesn't want to be alone."

I get up and walk to the kitchen.

"Oh, Mardi, do you want some *du ris au lait?*" Grand-mère finally sees me. She's smiling, already pouring some pudding into the ceramic strawberry bowl I made last year in art class.

I nod.

"Answer your grandmother with your lips," says my mother. "What are you? A mute?" She's half teasing me.

"I want it!" Pélé says.

"Aaahhh! You see? He was hungry! Here you go, sweetheart." She gives him my bowl. Everyone nods, yes, that's it, he's hungry and he doesn't want to be alone. But there's more to it than what they think. Uncle Perrin pats me on my arm and winks at me. I move away from him.

"Do you still practice your French?" he asks me.

"No."

"Why not?"

"I don't know why."

"Pierre and Patrick are taking private lessons," says Mr. LeBalle.

"Yes," says Pierre. *"Je suis, tu es, il est, vous êtes, nous sommes, ils sont."*

Patrick looks at his shoes.

"Mardi knows her English much better now." Serina smiles. "She's just lazy when it comes to the French."

"Mardi's not lazy," my father says, pouring himself another glass of rum. "She very smat girl," he continues in English. "She do goot in school, eh?"

"Yes, she is smart," my mother says. "She scored one hundred on one of her exams. Didn't she show you?"

They all have something to say about me except me.

What I think?

I think the last time I checked the mirror, I was there.

"Thank you," I say to the critics in the kitchen. "Thank you all." I take my bowl of *du ris au lait* and go into the bathroom.

I flush it down the toilet.

My favorite Saturday-morning show is *The Gang Is Here*. It's about a group of high school kids living in California trying to put together a rock band. Every week something goes wrong: either Jennifer accidentally glues her lips together, Rick has laryngitis, or Lauren hurts her knee and can't dance in the talent show where a big record producer will be and the band can't do the number without her.

I like all that drama.

Everyone on *The Gang Is Here* looks like they don't belong in this world; they're just teasing us on planet Earth before they fly off to whatever place good-looking people come from. The girls on the show are pretty, thin, never wear the same clothes twice, have their own rooms, and date by the time they're twelve. The boys look just as good, and they worship the girls. When things go wrong, they go to the beach to think and sing a song. When they return home, everything is all right again—in half an hour.

We all sleep late on Saturday mornings, so this is the only time I get the TV to myself. I jump out of bed. There isn't a TV in the bedroom. Aunt Widza, thinking our TV was a plant, poured water in it. The TV sparked like a firecracker, then went blank, like Aunt Widza's eyes when she saw what she had done.

After brushing my teeth I go into the kitchen. The clock on the wall with Jesus Christ at His Last Supper says 6:30. I don't even wake up this early for school. I take a bowl, milk, and a box of Rice Krispies cereal and move to the living room.

Then I see Uncle Perrin and Pélé. Pélé is still asleep, but Uncle Perrin is up taping the head of his guitar.

"Hey, Biskwit." He looks up, smiling at me. I forgot how white and straight his teeth are. I used to make him laugh so I could see the deep dimples in his cheeks.

"You didn't bring any food for your uncle?"

"No." I turn on the TV. I push aside his floor bed and set everything down on the carpet. As I eat, he twangs away on his guitar.

All my favorite shows come on, but it's not the same.

Pélé wakes up, stretching and yawning.

"*Ti Pélé!*" Uncle Perrin says. "Here's my little man."

"*Bonjou,* Papa Perrin," Pélé says to him, and to me: "*Bonjou* . . . Wednesday?"

Uncle Perrin laughs.

"My name is Tuesday," I correct Pélé.

"Oh." He sits quietly for a while, looking at the TV.

Then I realize he's not really looking at the TV; although he's facing the set, he's somewhere else. I watch him. His mouth opens halfway and he starts drooling.

"Pélé!" Uncle Perrin snaps his finger. Pélé shakes his head and wakes up.

"Does he always do that?" I ask.

"Sometimes he gets disoriented," Uncle Perrin says. "And sometimes he's sleeping with his eyes open."

"How old is he?"

"Five."

"My birthday is on . . . Tuesday!" Pélé laughs. He's missing his two top and bottom teeth.

"Mazora!" I call him, a name for people who lose their teeth. But Pélé's not offended. He covers his mouth and continues laughing.

"Why did they let you keep him?" I ask Uncle Perrin.

"I told immigration I was his stepfather."

"They believed you? You didn't have anything to prove it."

"Pélé, go brush your teeth," Uncle Perrin says to him. "When you're done I'll make you breakfast, whatever you like." After Pélé runs to the bathroom, Uncle Perrin puts his guitar down and faces me. "Do you remember your grandmother's yard, the section where she kept the animals?"

I nod.

"Remember when it rained, how muddy it got, and the chickens, the goat, stray cats and dogs, rats, and flies would all go inside that little wooden house, and it was crowded, smelly, with the roof barely keeping them dry?"

I nod again.

"That was us in a boat on the Atlantic before the Coast Guard found us, and that was us living in the refugee camps. Pélé and his mother were the only relief I had. The only way they would keep us together is if we said we were a family. Pélé's mother had some distant relatives living somewhere in the United States. Immigration said they would look for them, so this is going to be temporary."

"Suppose they don't find anyone?"

"Then I have a son and you have a new cousin."

Pélé comes back and sits on the floor next to me.

I get up to go rinse my bowl. As I'm putting the milk back in the refrigerator, my father walks in. He has on the black-and-white striped pajamas I gave him for Christmas last year. My mother says he looks like a convict from an old movie, but my father told her he liked them fine.

"You always up in morning, huh? Watch TV?" Papa says in his broken English. "You fee-neesh 'omework?"

He asks me this question every Saturday and every Saturday I answer "Yes."

"Goood gel?"

"Yes."

"Ah, yes!" He smiles and pats me on the head like a puppy. I like my father's smile except for his half-golden front tooth. He thinks it's sexy. He had it done in Haiti for his twenty-second birthday, and all the girls back then liked it. It's so old-style Haitian.

"Mardi, you make-a coffee for Dah-dee?" he asks, looking for something at the stove. "Huh? Where coffee, huh?"

"Papa, I don't know how to make that kind of coffee using the old pot," I say, rinsing my bowl and the pots left soaking in the sink. "We should buy one of those automatic coffee makers."

"Coffee no taste-a same," he says, looking for the aluminum coffeepot. Then in Créole he says: "I don't like that watered-down liquid they call coffee in this country. For the coffee to be coffee, the grounds must boil in the water, not have water pass through them."

"The electric coffee maker is *plis fasile.*"

"What is easy?" my mother asks, walking in.

"Nothing," I say quickly.

"I heard what you said," she says.

Then why do you ask? I scrub my pot harder and faster.

"Wash the stove, too," she tells me, taking out a jar of Jif crunchy peanut butter. She sits down at the kitchen table with a knife and a piece of cassava. I grab a Brillo pad and start cleaning the stove. While she crunches on the cassava, I scrub, and my father flips through his newspaper, *Nouvelle Haitian.*

"I went into Manhattan yesterday," my mother says, "to fill out applications at the Holiday Inn and Parker Meridien hotels. They said they would call, but I don't know, Henri."

"We should get an answering machine in case they call when we're not here," says my father.

"And have the credit card companies leaving messages?"

"You're right."

"Maman," I say, "you should open your own restaurant. Everyone is always telling you to do that. You should call it Polette's Passion."

"Hah!" says my mother. "I'm too old, I have no money, and I don't trust anyone."

I know nothing is easy except dreaming, but even *that* my mother won't do. I look out the window. Sun so warm but it's millions of miles away from here. There's this hanging toy made of colored glass dangling by the window. I found it at the reusable-things yard and it has animal shapes in a circle. I think it's one of those things they put above a baby in a crib. The sun shines through it, putting a dancing monkey on the tiled kitchen floor. Next is a kangaroo with a baby in its pouch. I had a blue purse in Haiti with all these animals on it that my mother brought me on one of her visits. Every time I opened the purse, it sang a song, "Flower Duet." The name was written on the back of the purse. Seeing the dancing animals on the floor, I start to hear that song and it takes me to that trip in the countryside, the trip we all went on, when Serina taught me how to float and Maman and Papa laughed their heads off whenever I told them a joke. On the ride back I opened the purse and stuck it out the window so it could sing, and the wind blew it out of my hand. But I still hear the song inside my purse:

Traaa da da la, Traaa da da la, Tra da da da lala lala lalalalala lala lala . . .

Uncle Perrin walks in and the song stops. "So what do you people want to eat?" he asks, opening the refrigerator. "I'm cooking this morning."

"Oh, Perrin," my mother says. "Sit down. Rest."

"Don't you know Perrin is a man who doesn't like to sit down?" Papa says. "When he was a baby he learned to run before he could crawl. This is what keeps getting him into trouble, jumping steps and not following rules."

"Trust me, big brother," says Uncle Perrin, "when I'm tired of standing I'll sit." Papa is old enough to be Uncle Perrin's father. He was eighteen years old when Uncle Perrin was born. Aunt Widza came a few years after that.

Uncle Perrin takes food from the refrigerator: *batata*, yuca, onions, eggs, green plantains, sausage, ham, and a box of spaghetti from the pantry. He places everything on the table.

"You're cooking all that?" Maman laughs. "A real chef. Sit down while Mardi finishes with the stove." Then she notices a box of Rice Krispies sticking out of the garbage. "*Mezanmi!* That's the third box of cereal this week I've had to buy. What do you children do with the food? Are you feeding your friends?"

I'm guilty. I made Rice Krispies Treats all this week.

"Listen," she continues, "there are other people who eat cereal in this house."

"Well," Papa says, "if that's what Mardi likes to eat, then—"

"Then nothing, Henri! I'm not telling people to die of starvation but to learn how to make things last. Don't you know last week I went to buy underwear and I couldn't afford it?"

"Because you buy fifty-dollar panties," I say under my breath.

"What did you say?" she asks.

She pauses, waiting for me. I pretend I'm too busy with the stove to be bothered.

"*Reponn mwen non, frekan!* Answer me, fresh girl!" Maman's words hit me like a glass ball. I shake my head, trying to get the invisible sharp pieces out of my hair, letting the hot water turn my palms red.

"Oh, Polette," Uncle Perrin says, "Mardi's young. She's not a bad child."

"Thanks to me she not any worse," says Maman. "She was in such a state when she first got here."

Maman is right. I was in a state when I got here. Serina and I came one week and two weeks later we started school. I didn't want to do anything except sit in a corner. It had been a long time since Serina and I lived with our mother and father.

I believed they were happy to see us when we lived in Port-au-Prince, but not then, not when we were earlier than they expected. They had no smiles for us when they went to pick us up at the New York airport, no gifts. "More mountains to climb after you thought you'd climbed your last one," my father had said. I knew that even before my father said it. I knew that right at Kennedy Airport when my mother, Serina, and I were outside with our luggage waiting for my father to bring the van around. It was night and I was cold even though people were walking around without jackets on. I smelled gasoline; there were cars and buses everywhere, just like on the Delmas Route in Port-au-Prince. All I saw were highways and headlights. Not one mountain in sight, but I felt they were there. Only here, the mountains tend to be invisible.

I don't know about Serina, but I was expecting Maman and Papa to live in a big East Side apartment like the

Jeffersons on TV. Instead, the day we arrived they took us to this one-room apartment lit by only one lightbulb in a ceiling socket. That first night I heard them whispering. My mother was crying. "Shhh . . . shhh . . . , " Papa kept telling her. The shadows in the room were moving, telling me with their foggy fingers to come join them on the wall. I was so afraid I held on tightly to Serina, as tightly as I could without choking her.

Now, at the sink, the water is too hot. I cry out.

"What's the matter?" All three of them—Maman, Papa, and Uncle Perrin—get out of their seats, ready to come to me. But I don't want anybody.

"The water just got too hot," I say.

"Did you burn?" my mother asks.

"No." I turn the cold water back on. They sit back down again.

Hah! I made them jump.

"Mardi, hurry up with that stove and *s'il vous plaît* pay attention to what you're doing," Maman says. "Look at all those marks on your legs and arms. Today hot water, tomorrow who knows what, and the police will be in my face asking if I did it."

I keep quiet, enjoying the cool water on my hands this time. Uncle Perrin stands next to me, chopping the ham into tiny pieces.

"Are you sure you're not hurt?" he whispers.

"My skin is as thick as a crocodile's," I whisper back. I feel him watching me but I continue scrubbing to the beat of my blue purse song.

Late Saturday morning Jilline and I are walking on
Clarendon Road, heading toward Papa's yard on Utica Avenue. We've teamed up for a science report at school.
We're going to do it on solar energy and we need materials
to build a solar house. It was my idea. We're going to the
yard to look for scraps of wood, metal, cardboard, and
anything else we can find.

There are prizes this year, and first-prize winners get to
go away to this science camp for one month—free! I may
be too old to get excited about camp, but I want to win this
thing—I want to win something! My mother will probably
say no, but I'll worry about that after I win. I'm sure I'll
win. Everyone else is doing reports that they can only
show on paper. I'm going to leave them with something
they can touch and feel.

As Jilline talks on and on about her hair, nails, and

whatever, I smile, thinking about all the fun I'll have at a camp. When a chilly breeze hits my chest, I zip up my jacket. I look over at Jilline in hers, brown suede with black buttons. I really like it. Her grandfather gave it to her last year for her birthday. She also got matching boots, a purse, and a vest, which she's not wearing now.

What I think?

I think Mr. Hunter spoils Jilline. Not that that's bad if you're the one being spoiled, but Jilline doesn't care as much about her things as I do. Last Christmas her grandfather gave her a thirty-two-inch TV for her room. Two months later she dropped it on the floor and cracked the screen when she tried to rearrange her bedroom. The year before that she got a stereo system. But she blew out the speakers when she turned the volume up too high.

I guess her grandfather spoils her because she's the only grandchild he has. Jilline's father was Mr. Hunter's only child. Jilline tells me both her mother and father were drug addicts. They were driving high one night and got killed when they ran into a truck. Jilline was in the car and she was only six years old.

Jilline's jacket is very pretty. I'm feeling okay walking next to her because I have on my sister's black leather jacket. Serina had it on layaway for six months. She went to work early today and doesn't know I'm wearing it. Neither does my mother, who hates the jacket. She says it makes me look like I belong in a gang. When she saw it on me this morning, she made me take it off. Instead she gave me Grandmère's yellow sweater with green ducks and a blue hat with cartoons of dancing pumpkins. Once I got outside, though, I took her stuff off and slipped on what I wanted to wear.

"Hey, isn't that your sister?" Jilline is pointing across the street at Dudley's West Indian Record Shop.

I blink twice to make sure I'm seeing what I'm seeing. Serina is kissing a boy! In broad daylight! How could she be so stupid and brave at the same time? Somebody could see her and go tell Maman—somebody like me.

"Looks like your sister gets around," Jilline says, grinning.

Looks like I'm going to make some money. I know the boy Serina's kissing. His name is Jean-something and he goes to the same church we do. I've seen him talking to Serina after mass.

"Let's go surprise her." Jilline starts crossing the street.

"No." I hold her back. "I'll get her later." I don't want Serina to see me with her jacket on. We keep walking.

"So how long is your uncle staying?" Jilline asks.

"It looks like a long time. Him and that boy."

"Oh, that's so cute. I wish I had a little brother. I'd dress him up mad cool. All the little girls'd be clocking my little bro."

"Let's trade. I be you and you be me."

"I don't want to be you."

"Why not?"

"Look at you. You don't even have cable or your own room. It's not your fault, but a woman's got to have her privacy."

"But I'm not a woman. And you're not a woman."

"Yet." Jilline continues talking, reminding me about all

64

the "mad crazy dope" things she has or will have by the end of the year. I wonder if she realizes she's bragging again. But she is right. A girl's got to have her privacy. There are three other people in the room I sleep in. It wouldn't be so bad if they were all my age because then it would be like a slumber party that never ended.

"Hey, Mardi, here comes Ike."

I stop walking. Ike is coming at us—at me!—again.

"Don't be so afraid of him."

"I—I'm not."

He reaches us. "Hey, Jilline." That smile. That same one he had when he tripped me down the stairs.

"Hey, Ike," Jilline says, more out of politeness since she doesn't look so terribly pleased to see him, either. "What you doing here?"

"I live here, too, you know. I got a right to be out."

"Didn't say you didn't."

"Yeah, whatever. I'm just on a stroll, see? Looking for something to do." All the while he's looking from Jilline to me. Jilline stares back at him. I look at the ground.

After a moment Jilline says, "Well, we gotta go. See ya." We walk three blocks before I turn to look behind me. Ike is still in the same spot, all dressed in denim blue except for his red cap.

When we get to the yard, people are already there, digging and poking around in heaps of reusable things. We find my father arguing with a man over a tire.

"Good morning, Mr. Desravines," Jilline interrupts cheerfully.

"Ho, very goot morning to you, too, Gel-line." My

father smiles back. It's a good thing the sun isn't out yet or else his gold tooth could have blinded us.

"Hi." I wave.

"Your more-ther know you here?" he asks me.

Of course! Doesn't she always know where I am?

"Yes."

"What you two loo-king for?"

"Wha la!" the man with the tire yells with a West Indian accent. "You gon sell me dis ting or wha'?"

"Ey, lee-sen, I talking to my daughter," my father yells back. "If you not like price go other places." Papa takes me and Jilline by the shoulder and walks a few steps away. "Mardi, isn't that Serina's jacket?" he asks me in Créole.

"Yes," I say, speaking in English, not wanting to leave Jilline out.

"Didn't your mother tell you not to wear it?"

"She doesn't want me wearing it to school," I lie.

"Oh, it's a nice jacket. Someone might steal it if you go to school with it." Then he switches to English: "Anyway, why you two coming for here?"

Jilline begins to say something, but I cut her off. "We'll find it." I pull her away.

"Be careful, eh?"

"Don't worry," I say.

"Wha la, don' worry," the man with the tire yells to my father, "and be happy wit' the price I offer ya here."

After about an hour of looking all Jilline and I have found are mattress springs, hubcaps, and a few broken picture frames.

"Maybe today wasn't a good day to look," I say.

"What we looking for exactly?" Jilline finally asks, sitting down on a black-and-white polka-dot sofa.

"When we find it we'll know," I answer.

"Maybe we should change our report."

"No! I really want to build a house. It'll be fun. We can build a big house with lots of rooms and space and even make small furniture and trees."

"I'm not into all that. I just wanna get this over with," she says, picking something out of her nails. "Maybe we should just save this for an art class or something. Maybe we should do one of those volcano reports with vinegar and baking soda."

"That's so boring. All the boys always do that. I want to win first prize and leave for the summer." See, Jilline has her grandfather's rich family in South Carolina to go to. When I went outside this past summer, it was either to pray in empty churches with my grandmother or to walk Aunt Widza around Holy Cross Cemetery. Aunt Widza likes to make up stories about people buried there. She and Grandmère Adda never wanted to go anywhere else except those two places.

Even if I don't win this contest, I still want to do things next summer. I'd like to go swimming, take a trip to the Empire State Building, or even go to Coney Island. I didn't tell anyone in my family about the contest. I think Serina would back me up. Aunt Widza would be for me, but her opinion wouldn't count. In time I could get Papa on my side, but Grandmère and Maman would be mountains. They don't trust other people around me.

"Aaahhh! Children are delicate things," my

grandmother said when I wanted to go to a sleepover at Jilline's house. Everyone knows and likes Jilline in my family. We call her *ti Ameriken nwa*, the little black American. Jilline only lives a few blocks away, so I thought it would be okay to ask.

"Aaahhh! Children don't know when someone is putting poison in their ice cream," my grandmother had said. "I know what I talk about. When I was a young girl about your age in Jacmel, my best friend, Marie-Anne, died because she took a stranger's hand and went off into the woods. We found her body two days later by the river over in a nearby town under a mapou tree."

"I thought you said Haiti was a safe place when you and my mother were growing up," I pointed out.

"In the sweetest life you can find the most bitter tales," she said.

"All right," Jilline says, getting up to look in another pile, "but if we don't find anything else we have to do another report or buy one—" Jilline's eyes pop open.

"What?"

"Lookit this!" Jilline holds up a battered videocassette with naked women on the cover with breasts the size of watermelons. The title reads: *The Mighty Big Ones*.

Jilline smiles a smile, as my mother would say, wide enough for ships to pass through. I can see the clouds moving behind her head, making way for the sunshine that all of a sudden lights up the whole yard.

"Well," Jilline says, "I guess we won't be watching *The Sound of Music* for a while."

We? "What you, you going to do?"

"Take it home and hide it," she says matter-of-factly.

"Wh-why don't you jist—*just*—leave it alone?"

"Why? I'm not asking you to take it home. Unless you want to, Mardi." Jilline holds the tape to my face. I shake my head and back away as if she's offering me fire.

What I think?

I think God and eight policemen wouldn't be able to save me if my mother found me with that tape.

"No!" I say. "That's okay."

"That's what I thought." Jilline puts the tape in her bag. "I'll hold on to it, then." Sometimes I can't trust Jilline as much as I would like to. She's the kind of friend who would encourage me to get an A on a test but suggest I cheat just in case.

Jilline has to go do her hair, so we don't walk back home together. I'm carrying all the stuff we found at the yard since I'm the one who's going to build the foundation of "the house that didn't prove anything," as Jilline puts it. I also have some other small things I found that I know Pierre will like. I'm going to need money to buy materials for this report, like glue and construction paper. Maybe I'll let Pierre help. She's really good in art. Her drawings are always up on the bulletin board at school.

It's not until I see the Amorez Supermarket sign that I remember Maman giving me money to buy vinegar and sour oranges to clean the chicken we're cooking for tomorrow's Sunday meal. Maman believes in cleaning chicken, I mean *really* cleaning chicken. You'd think she's trying to bring the animal back to life, the way she rubs it with lemons and sour oranges and flips it up in the air like pizza dough so the spices sink in. That is so unnecessary. After all, here the meat's coming from a factory, not someone's backyard.

I'm about to go inside when I stop: Aunt Widza. I don't want her embarrassing me. But, no, it's okay. She's not working today.

I'm about to go inside again when this time my heart stops: The Mildred Rodriguez is in the store talking to Santos! She's smiling and tossing her hair when it's not even in her face. God is so mean. Every time I see her, I feel like nothing. Even with Serina's leather jacket on I don't feel cool anymore, especially not with all this . . . *junk* I'm carrying!

I can't go to the Associated Supermarket one block up because for one thing, Associated doesn't sell sour oranges. Second, it's more expensive. Maman gave me the exact change to go to the Amorez Supermarket.

Thank goodness Mildred and Santos walk off to the back. I run in and get the vinegar and the oranges.

"Aiy, mí señorita linda!" says Mr. Amorez, Santos's father. He's smiling at me when I go to one of the cash registers. He always calls me Little Miss Cutie. It used to make me feel special until I realized he says that to all the women and girls. I try to return his smile as I dig deep in my pockets and pull out dimes, nickels, and pennies.

The supermarket is packed. A few other people are waiting on line behind me now.

"Mira, Santos!" Mr. Amorez yells. "Coming to help me with the customers!"

When he says that, I drop half the change on the floor. Santos is coming!

The people on line help me pick the coins up and give them back to me.

"You missing twenty cents, *señorita,*" Mr. Amorez says after counting the change.

I don't know what to say. Everyone's looking at me.

"Yeah, Pop?" That's Santos behind me. Now I'm frozen.

"Don't worry, *señorita,*" Mr. Amorez says to me, "if the money on the floor, I find when I mop tonight."

I nod and hurry for the door, avoiding Santos and Mildred standing there.

"Ey, *ti madmwazèl,*" a woman on line calls out to me in Créole, "you're forgetting your things."

The bag with the vinegar and sour oranges is still at the counter! I grab it and rush out of the store.

I run down the block with the bag of junk banging against my leg. At the first garbage can I see, I dump the sour oranges in. I get to my building and run up the stairs. Patrick and his mother are coming down the stairs. He smiles but I barely say hello to them.

When I get home, I slam the front door. Then I listen for their voices. I don't hear Maman or Grandmère.

In the kitchen Serina is taking fat off some chicken and Aunt Widza is sitting down, pounding spices in the wooden mortar.

"It's about time you got back," Serina says. "Where are the oranges?"

"They were all rotten," I say, tight-lipped.

"Did you go shopping again?" Aunt Widza asks, eyeing the bags from the yard.

Serina begins to laugh. "Macy's had a junk sale."

Aunt Widza joins in.

"Shut up!" I say.

"What did you say to me?" Serina stops laughing and points the sharp cleaning knife at me.

"I saw you kissing that boy today and I'm going to tell!"

"What a lie," Serina says calmly. "I haven't left the house all day, and isn't that my jacket you have on?"

Oh, no. I forgot to take it off.

"I'm not stupid! It was . . . Jean-Robert you were kissing in front of the record shop this morning!" I yell at her. I would never raise my voice to anyone if I knew my mother and grandmother were around.

Aunt Widza laughs harder.

"No one's calling you stupid, stupid," Serina says.

Aunt Widza is falling off her chair. "I–I thought I was the only s-stupid one here! Is someone taking over my job?"

Serina looks over at her and starts to laugh again. They're like sisters, and a small part of me wants to laugh, too, and be where they are.

"Both of you are stupid and should shut up!" I run out of the kitchen.

"Oh, you little *bébé* lala . . . ," I hear Serina saying behind me.

I go into the room and slam another door. I grab a puzzle from the closet and the Walkman off Serina's bed. I throw off my coat and shoes and climb up to my bed. I wish I could throw things around, but the most I can do is dump the puzzle pieces on my bed and run my hands through them like I'm looking for something. I find a green piece the shape of an amoeba and begin. I bend my neck forward so my head won't hit the cold, cracked ceiling.

I put the headphones on and turn the volume up high on the Nina Bastien tape in the Walkman. Nina is talking to me. She's saying: "Don't you know nothin' bad stays bad forever? Don't you know a sting is a temporary thang?"

I fall asleep. When I wake up, the room is dark and I'm covered in puzzle pieces.

I'm hungry. I haven't eaten since I left to go to the yard with Jilline. I can smell the chicken cooking in the spices. I hear many different voices and Uncle Perrin twanging, trying to tune that guitar.

I get up and tiptoe to the bathroom. I don't turn on any lights because I don't want them to know I'm awake. I want to know what they talk about when they think I'm asleep.

I leave the bathroom door open a crack.

"Aaahhh! Don't get shampoo in my eyes! You want me to go blind?"

Twang. Twang.

"Pardon, Grandmère."

I guess Serina is washing Grandmère Adda's hair at the kitchen sink.

"Let me give you a perm," I hear Serina say.

"Aaahhh! All those chemicals in the perm seep through your head and make you have problems with your brain," Grandmère says.

"The world would be a safer place if people had simpler brains," says Aunt Widza.

Yeah, you would know.

"Perms can only damage what's on top of your head," my mother says, "not what's inside."

"That's not true," says my grandmother. "I remember a long time ago when I was still living in Jacmel–this was before Perrin and Widza were born–I was living next door to a woman who had a daughter. The daughter wanted her pubic hair to be soft so she gave herself a perm down there. She got sick and died two days later."

Twang. Twang.

"Oh, Grandmère Adda," Serina says, "that's impossible!"

"Believe me if you want," my grandmother says, "but it really happened." I can picture Grandmère pouting right now because no one, as usual, seems to believe her strange story. I don't think my grandmother knows any stories with princes and princesses, castles, rainbows, and fairies. Everyone dies at the end of her stories, and they almost always deserve it.

"Maman Adda," I hear my mother saying, "Serina shouldn't be hearing things like that. It might give the child ideas."

"I would never perm my hair down there," Serina says.

"That's not what I meant," my mother says. "If you're

thinking about doing one thing down there, most certainly you'll think about doing other things."

"Like sex?" Aunt Widza asks.

Twang. Twang.

I almost burst out laughing. It's quiet for a moment. Then Aunt Widza begins singing "I Want Your Sex."

"Stop that, Widza!" says my mother. "Stop being silly!"

Aunt Widza stops singing. She and Serina are laughing.

"Why are you grinning like a fat cat?" my mother asks.

"Oh, nothing," I hear Serina say.

"What do you know about sex?"

"Oh, nothing."

Just then I hear something move inside the bathtub. I close the door and turn on the lights. I slowly walk to the tub and pull back the curtains. Pélé is sleeping there, covered with my blanket. I wonder what would happen if I turned on the cold water. But I stop smiling when I see him sucking his thumb and shivering. I pick him up and carry him to the living room sofa. As I cover him with a blanket, I think about the question my mother asked Serina.

"What do you know about sex?"

I'd hate for my mother to ask me that question. If she asked me, I couldn't lie to her.

Twang. Twang.

The whole family is going to church this Sunday because of Uncle Perrin. Maman, Grandmère, and Aunt Widza are the ones who always go to St. Joseph's. Every now and then when Serina or I act up, they make us all go, even my father.

"I want to introduce you to our church here, and *la kominote*," my mother told Uncle Perrin.

"The community? With pleasure," he said.

I smell spices cooking. I hear Rainbow Radio, the Haitian AM radio station that only broadcasts on Sundays. They call themselves "the colorful station," but right now they're saying how a U.S. Coast Guard ship found two hundred Haitian refugees drowned in the Atlantic Ocean somewhere between Miami and Cuba. The six or seven people who didn't drown said their boat had split in two after fighting broke out. I can't imagine what it must be like to be floating and gasping in water deeper than three Empire State Buildings on top of each other. Must be what butterflies feel like when they're fluttering around in glass jars knowing they're about to die.

I'm glad to have woken up when I did because the rocks in my bed didn't work last night. It was a short dream, but still, the man with the machete was chasing me through the tall cornfields again. His machete had blood on it, and I wondered if the blood was mine or someone else's. It's been a while since I've had that dream. I'll never tell anyone about that or anything else. No one knows about the soldiers and the other two women I saw in the cornfields that morning when I was lost. My mother says, some things you give and some things you keep even when you're gone and buried deep in the ground.

Grandmère Adda and I are the first ones dressed for church. Pélé is also in the living room, playing with building blocks my father found in the yard. He's putting blocks on top of blocks, building a colorful square mountain. I must admit he looks a *little* cute in the suit my mother bought him.

I look at my grandmother cleaning under her nails with a toothpick, humming along to an old French song playing on Rainbow Radio.

"Aaahhh, look how lovely you are." Grandmère looks up at me.

"I look like a little girl," I say. I have on a dress Serina stopped wearing when she was ten. It's pink and frilly with a big bow at the waist on the back. I look like Pollyanna.

"Be happy you've got something nice to wear," Grandmère tells me. "You're lucky your mother buys you children good-quality things. If you're careful with that dress you can even save it for your own daughter to wear someday. Wouldn't that be nice?"

"I don't think so, Grandmère."

Uncle Perrin walks in. Like me, he's dressed in someone else's clothes—my father's, which are too big for him. "Look at Mardi," he says. "Look how pretty she is."

I roll my eyes.

"Aaahhh! That's what I told her, but she's not accepting compliments this morning."

"What?" he says, faking amazement. "Not accepting compliments? Is it true? Well, Mardi, dry earth has to soak up the rain at some point, or else it'll crack and blow away in the wind."

A song with a mellow guitar rhythm and a hard pounding beat booms out of the radio. Uncle Perrin begins to dance, twisting his body this way and that. "Now, this is good music." He turns the volume up and grabs Grandmère. "Let's dance, *chérie!*"

"Aaahhh! Let go of me, boy!" Grandmère yells playfully. "You want me to fall?"

"Fall for the music, fall for love," Uncle Perrin says to her.

"You're asking for a beating!" But Grandmère gets up. Soon she's into the music, too, and does a few of her own moves. She looks like a dancing chicken, but a happy one. *"Ti Pélé,"* she says. "Come show Grandmère how you dance." But Pélé shakes his head and continues building his colorful mountain.

"I'll dance with you!" I say, but before I can make a move, my father comes out and tells everyone it's time to go. Uncle Perrin clicks off the radio. He winks at me and says, "Some other time, Biskwit, we'll dance all you want." I suddenly feel silly. I jumped up to dance too quickly. I should have sat where I was. Now he knows I'm not always angry.

The church is packed—and hot. Even though it's almost winter, the weather feels like summer.

"We are so sorry for the condition in the church," Father Wilson is saying, "but last week our fans were stolen. Your generous donations during offertory will help provide the church with new ones."

"Who would steal a fan from a church?" Maman whispers.

"Religious crackheads," Serina says. She and Grandmère are on one side of me and Aunt Widza and Pélé are on the other. Uncle Perrin, Papa, and Maman are in the row in front of us. Uncle Perrin's head has been bowed and he's been moving his lips since the service began.

Aunt Widza is sitting all through the mass because Pélé is asleep on her lap. I swallow a lump in my throat when she kisses him.

I feel better when the young dancers come out dressed

in colorful pants, scarves, and flowing skirts. A man beats on bamboo drums and others play wooden instruments. Four men and four women in white sing *"Pran Kouraj"*—"Take Courage"—as the young kids dance. Even Pierre LeBalle dances. And here she comes . . . and a-one, and a-two, and a—

Pierre trips and falls!

Thank you, Pierre! Patrick and his mother are in the next aisle. I catch his eye; we hold back our laughs. Pierre gets back up on her feet, finishes her dance, then takes a bow as if she's the star and this is her moment. But after the applause church returns to boring business.

I see two older boys smiling at me. Then I realize that it's not me they're looking at, it's Serina. Serina smiles back and even gives them a bonus wink. She had a lot of secret boyfriends in Haiti. Two of them came and cried at our gate the day before we left. She used to give me two *gouds,* forty cents, to deliver her love letters. Now I charge her a dollar. And next year, if her love life gets more complicated, I'll charge her two dollars.

I look around the large church again. This time, up. The ceiling is high and comes together like the tip of an ice cream cone from a machine. The stained-glass windows are so bright this morning I think the sun is sitting right behind them. I expect the pictures in the window to come to life any second. The statues of Saint This and Saint That seem to have their feet on fire, with all the lighted candles below them.

Everyone is dressed up as if they're going to a big wedding: hair freshly permed, weaves and extensions in place, suits pressed, shoes shiny, and each woman with enough makeup on to open her own beauty supply store.

This is different from the English mass, where I see people in jeans and a T-shirt.

"I don't see anything wrong with that," I once said in front of Maman, Papa, and Grandmère. "As long as they have on clean clothes."

"What!" the three shouted together.

"You see that, Henri?" my mother said to my father. "I wouldn't be surprised if this child showed up in torn jeans and a bra made of safety pins at her own wedding!"

Now I smile at the idea of my wedding, me in jeans and a bra. And what would Santos, my husband-to-be, wear? No shirt, Timberland boots, and oversized Gap jeans. Then I notice Uncle Perrin watching me. I lower my eyes, take a deep breath, and coldly stare back. He shakes his head and faces the altar again.

Victory.

I smile.

Then I realize that I shouldn't be grinning. This is the special one-year anniversary mass for the group of women who were killed last year in a bus accident. The women belonged to St. Joseph's and they were returning from a bus trip to Atlantic City. One woman had won twenty-five thousand dollars and was going to put a down payment on a house with the money.

They say the driver of the car that hit them was drunk.

Relatives of these women hold white flowers in their hands. I look over at Pierre and her father, who are in the same row now as Patrick and his mother. Pierre is crying.

Her mother used to perm my mother's and sister's hair. She was round like the moon, with a laugh loud as thunder.

Mrs. LeBalle was one of the women on the bus.

I face the altar. Father Wilson is wiping the goblet clean. He kisses the altar table—a sign that the mass is ending. I bow my head and say my special prayer: Please help me be a good girl. Please keep all the bad things away, when I'm awake and when I'm sleeping.

I seal my prayer with the sign of the cross. Some people are still kneeling from Holy Communion. My mother and father are deep in prayer. They hold each other's hand. I wonder sometimes what they pray for, but I feel like they don't want the same things I do.

Where have I been all this time? I've missed communion.

Later that day, while Serina is braiding my hair and humming along with her favorite *kompa* CD on the radio, I sit on the floor between her legs, trying to write her college essay.

"Make me sound really good, Biskwit," she says. She dips her finger in a jar of Dax pomade and gently spreads it on my scalp. Her finger feels like water, and if I'm not careful the rhythm of her breathing could make me fall asleep. I relax against her legs.

"This is not hard at all," I tell her. "All this college wants to know is why you want to come to their school and study. So why do you?"

"Stop moving your head. Like I told you, it's a good school, it's not expensive, and they have a good nursing program. Oh, and also, they're building a big mall right by it."

I wrote exactly what she said, except for the mall thing.

"Okay, good. Why the nursing program?"

"Because it'll pay good money when I graduate."

"No, besides that. Give me something deeper, like why do you really want to be a nurse?"

"Oh." She stops braiding my hair and thinks for a moment. "Oh! I know why!" She continues braiding, excited. "Remember how when I was little I used to pretend my dolls were sick and besides making them nice clothes to wear I would also make sure they took their medication to get better?" Again, I write and then rewrite.

"I loved doing that, do you remember, Mardi?"

"Yes," I answer. I do remember. Serina would never let me near her dolls, especially when they were "sick," and a doll could get sick if she left it outside for too long, if it fell in the mud, or if a dog peed on it. And medication was baby powder.

"And when I was in the cornfields," she continues, "I saved a little boy's life."

I put my pen down. "What?"

"Remember when we were on our way to the airport and those people started shooting at us and we all had to hide in the cornfields—"

"Yes, yes, I remember! I'll always remember!"

She hesitates, surprised by the sudden change in my

mood. "Well, that morning you had gone—without anyone's permission—to look for water, I saved a little boy's life."

"How could you do that?"

"Well, he somehow swallowed a rock and started choking. I was the one who got behind him and pushed his stomach and made him throw it up. Yeah, I did. Can we put that in?"

I start writing again, not leaving anything out.

"Why are you so quiet now?" she asks.

"Nothing," I answer.

"You mad about something?"

"Ow!" I hold my head and turn around. "You're pulling my hair!"

"Sorry. Your hair isn't even as tangled as it usually is." She finishes braiding my hair and I finish writing her essay in silence. I hand her the paper.

"It's all there," I tell her. "You said it all, and all you have to do is type it up. You don't have to pay me."

She pulls the dead strands of my hair from her comb. "You won't take money now? I'll pay you. I don't mind. I said I would." She reaches over to the radio and takes out the *kompa* CD, turning up the volume to this hip-hop station. My father bangs on the wall.

"Turn your music down, *s'il te plaît!*"

Serina rolls her eyes and lowers the volume. "If I was playing Tabou Combo he wouldn't be complaining."

"I don't want your money," I say, opening the bedroom door. Before I leave, I turn to her. "You should be a doctor, Serina. If you think you can save lives you should at least get the highest degree in it."

84

She looks at me curiously. I don't think she's ever had that idea before.

In the living room, Pélé is playing with his colorful blocks. Uncle Perrin is sitting on the sofa's edge. Aunt Widza is across from him with an open notebook in her lap.

"Yes, I wrote down all the songs we used to sing," she's telling Uncle Perrin. "Remember the one about Malice and Bouki and the eight days?" She starts to sing and Uncle Perrin's guitar tries its best not to sound broken. Aunt Widza always had a nice singing voice, and after a while the guitar strangely sounds fresh and light, but strong–like a cracked bell ringing. Uncle Perrin closes his eyes and hums as Aunt Widza sings:

"Oh, yes, Malice is a trickster,
He is, he is, Bouki cried.
Told me he'd be back to untie me
Eight days to the next Tuesday
But he lied, he lied.
Years have passed, and
Here I am still roped to this tree
While Malice is off riding my goat.
Will anyone remember me?"

Today I think my heart will stop. Santos blew me a kiss. That's not what I prayed for in church but it's just as good.

Santos blew me three kisses today! First one was in the morning in English class. We were taking a test, so everyone's eyes were on their paper. My eyes were also on the back of his head. I saw him make sure Mrs. Orlando wasn't looking. He glanced at The Mildred Rodriguez, who was smelling and playing with her hair, then slowly turned around, setting his eyes on me. I quickly looked away. When I tried to sneak another look at him, he was still staring at me.

Then he did it, blew a silent kiss to me, and turned back to his paper.

I didn't move. Couldn't. Maybe he meant the kiss for someone behind me?

The second kiss: Santos came into the lunchroom and sat directly across from me at the next table. He didn't even have a tray. He put his elbows on the table, resting his chin in his hands, staring at me again. This time I couldn't doubt it because there wasn't anyone around me. I tried to eat my lunch, pretending that the dried meat loaf and the soupy mash potatoes were more interesting than him.

I finally faced him and he blew me another kiss. Someone was pounding a serious drum in my chest.

Then, just as quick as he had sat down, Santos got up and left the lunchroom.

Kiss three: at the end of the day when I was leaving school. I passed by his locker and he did it again. Then he went:

"*Pssst. Pssst.*"

I pretended I didn't hear.

"*Pssst!* Yo, why you always in a hurry? I wanna talk to you."

I kept walking.

"Yo! Your aunt work in my father's store."

Oh, no, I thought. What's Aunt Widza done now? I knew we should never have let her work!

This time I had to stop and turn around.

"What's up?" Santos said seriously.

I nodded. The hallway was full of kids rushing out of school. They were shoulder-bumping me and knocking my knapsack off left and right.

"So why don't you ever say hello to me? You know me. I know your aunt. I didn't know she was your aunt. She real . . . nice, and funny."

Nice? Funny? Not bad.

He was about to say something else when I saw The Mildred Rodriguez walking up to us. She was looking at me the same way I looked at Uncle Perrin. I turned to run and got another shock: Ike was standing right behind me. One corner of his mouth was turned up in a quarter-moon smile. He reached out for me but I ducked and ran out of school.

Now I'm at home sitting at the kitchen table. I'm breathing hard because I ran the twelve blocks home. I take out Malice and scribble: *Hey, when did you become a butterfly? Maybe Aunt Widza working at the supermarket isn't such a bad idea.* I trace my lips with my fingers and laugh out loud.

"What's so funny, Biskwit?" Uncle Perrin comes in with Pélé right behind him. That's Pélé's thing now, to follow Uncle Perrin everywhere he goes and to imitate everything he does.

Uncle takes a pitcher out of the refrigerator. "Want some lemonade? Why are you breathing so hard?"

"Hey, you," says Pélé, "why are you breathing so hard?"

"Oh, shut up!" I tell Pélé.

"You shut up!" he says.

"No, *you* shut up!" I say back.

"Shut your *cric-crac* before I break it!" he yells at me. I'm so surprised that for a moment I don't know what to say.

"Both of you stop that!" says Uncle Perrin. "Mardi, at your age you can't be fighting with someone as young as Pélé."

"Oh, leave me alone," I say.

"Don't talk to me like that," he says. "I'm older than you. I could be your father."

"Yes, you could be, but you're not my father." I'm trembling as I say the words.

But Uncle Perrin stands looking at me. I stare right back at him.

"*Mon Dye,* Mardi." He calmly shakes his head. "My God, Mardi, you have changed. Ever since I got here you've treated me like I did something wrong to you. I notice how you ignore me, how you hold your breath and roll your eyes every time I come next to you. Tell me what's the matter so I can fix it."

"You can't fix anything," I tell him. "You're too late."

An hour later I'm at the library. I didn't plan on being here to work on my science report, but I didn't want to stay home with Uncle Perrin. So far I've been the only one working on the report. Every time I try to talk with Jilline about it she says we have lots of time since the report isn't due until spring. So I started without her. But instead of concentrating, I'm looking out the window. A pile of books on solar energy is stacked in front of me. I've only been through two books and written three sentences. Now I feel stupid for what I said to Perrin. Oh, I meant it, but what if he tells Maman?

I write in Malice: *Damn*. I feel Malice's smooth, cold cover and flip through his pages. Maybe I should have called my notebook Bouki instead. In the stories that Grandmère used to tell me, Bouki is the dumb one Malice always plays his tricks on.

I put Malice away. I rip up the page with the three sentences I've written into tiny pieces. Then I try to put them all together again.

"Heyyy, island guuurl."

My head is down but I know who it is.

"You too good to talk, talk to me? Hey, island guuurl, guess who?"

I look up. Ike's eyes are shiny red. He's breathing as hard and angry as a stabbed bull.

"What, you not gonna talk to me? You talk to other boys at school." He sits down across from me. I move my chair back.

"H-hi."

"Thas better. Whatchu doing?"

"B-books."

He looks through the pile. "You's a nerd. Like my muther was. So, so you like science?"

"B-books, for projeek—*project*."

"Uh-huh." He picks up a book on electricity and throws it to the other end of the long table. "I hate all this—"

"Can I help you, Isaac?" Jilline's grandfather walks up. I'm so glad to see him.

"S-step off, man!" Ike shouts at Mr. Hunter. "This ain't about you!"

"You are in my library and if—"

"Your library? I don't see your name on it. How you gonna *own* a library? I go to the supermarket and they throw me out. I come here and you wanna do the same thing."

"Isaac, you're disturbing everyone in here with your behavior!" Mr. Hunter whispers loudly. He steps closer to Ike and sniffs him. "Boy, you've been drinking?"

"You asking me or accusing me again?"

Mr. Hunter sighs. "Isaac, come into my office. Let me help you, son, let's talk."

"Ain't got time," Ike says, getting up. "Ain't nobody's son." He looks at me like I'm to blame. Then he pins that moon grin on his face.

"Nope, Ike ain't got no more time," he says, walking out of the library.

Mr. Hunter shakes his head. I finally breathe out.

Ike is not outside the library when I leave, thank God. When I get home, Pierre is sitting in the living room watching *Mary Poppins* with Aunt Widza and Grandmère.

"*Bonjou,* Grandmère. *Bonjou,* Matant. Where's Uncle Perrin and Pélé?"

"Hi, Mardi," Pierre answers in English. "Your father and mother drove them to go visit some people that could be Pélé's family."

Finally, some good news.

"What are you doing here?" I ask Pierre, taking my coat off.

"Patrick and his mother had to go out. When I got here you already left for the library, so I waited. You want to go play in your room? I brought my Monopoly."

"I hate Monopoly."

"I have my *osle*."

"I stopped playing Haitian jacks a long time ago."

"Aaahhh, stop talking," says Grandmère in Créole.

"Yes," adds Aunt Widza, "we can't hear what Mary is saying to the little children. Oh, Mardi, I saw your little friend again today at the supermarket."

"Jilline?" I ask.

"No, Mr. Amorez's son, Santos."

Oh . . . Oh . . . Something heavy is going to fall.

"He's going to be very handsome when he grows up. Do you like him, Mardi?"

"I don't think I know him," I say.

"Yeah, you do," Pierre says. "He's in our English class and sits in the front by Mildred Rodriguez. You're always looking at him."

"No I don't!"

"Okay, if you say so," says Pierre. God, I could smack her head against the wall!

"Well," Aunt Widza continues, "if I were Mardi I'd be in love, too. But I'd also be careful with that boy. He thinks he's a man." She looks straight at me and nods when she says this.

"Aaahhh, love," says Grandmère. "The only thing Mardi should be in love with now is her schoolwork. Men and boys and all the other things that go with them can wait. And what I'm saying goes for you, too, Pierre."

"*Oui*, Grandmère Adda," Pierre says. "So what do you want to do, Mardi? I've seen this movie already."

"Grandmère," I say, "can I go to Jilline's house?"

"What for?" she asks.

"She has some of my books that I need for homework." I'm not lying; I always lend Jilline my books so I can go to her house later and pick them up.

"You can go," Grandmère says, "but don't take long. Your mother will be home soon. You know she doesn't like you going to other people's houses." My mother believes people won't respect you and that they'll talk behind your back, do *tripotay,* if you go to their house too much. She says, "Never give people an opportunity to soak your name in the same tub they do their dirty laundry."

I put my coat on again and run to the bedroom to drop off the science books I borrowed from the library. When I get back to the front door, Pierre is waiting for me with her coat on.

"Let's go," she says.

"Oh, no," I say. "You're staying." I don't want to drag Pierre along. She would be all in my business. "*Mary Poppins* is a good movie, Pierre. I've seen it six times myself."

Pierre is about to cry. "*Mwen vle ale.* I wanna go," she says over and over in Créole so my grandmother can understand.

"Of course you're going, honey," Grandmère says to Pierre, "because if you don't go, Mardi won't go."

Pierre is as happy as a puppy. I push her out of the apartment and slam the front door.

It has started raining out and of course Pierre comes prepared with her big umbrella.

"It's good I came, huh?" she asks.

I don't answer her.

"I have an umbrella bigger than this that my mother has, but Patrick and his mother borrowed it. They had to go see a lawyer. I didn't feel like going with them. Patrick's mother is getting a divorce from his father but his father doesn't know it yet."

"Really?"

"Uh-huh."

"Are they going to live with you forever?"

"Maybe. I would like that."

We reach Jilline's house, a three-story brownstone her grandfather owns farther down on Newkirk Avenue. I press the first-floor buzzer.

"Who is it?" a squeaky voice asks from the intercom.

"It's me, Jilline!" I say, shivering from the cold.

"Me who?"

"Mardi!" I say.

"And Pierre!" Pierre adds.

"What's the password?"

"Stop playing, Jilline! It's raining!" I say.

"Okay," she says, but she doesn't buzz us in until a minute later.

Jilline is waiting for us at her front door with this boy named Kenny who's seventeen and lives on the second floor with his mother. When he sees Pierre and me coming, he kisses Jilline good-bye on the lips and runs upstairs without saying a word to us.

"Kenny came to fix my headphones," Jilline explains.

"Yeah, I bet he did," says Pierre under her breath.

"Isn't your grandfather home?" I ask. "I saw him at the library today."

"He won't be home till later. He's got some class he had to teach. Hi, Pierre. Y'all come on in."

The apartment smells like country-fresh Lysol. But the Lysol can't completely cover up the cigarette smoke underneath. Pierre and I sit down on the sofa. Jilline sits across from us on the La-Z-Boy. Pierre sees a bowl full of popcorn on the center table and smacks her lips loudly.

"Oh, where are my manners?" Jilline says, faking a Southern accent. "Help yourself to some homemade popcorn." I laugh, thinking of that same accent Jilline uses when she tells me stories of the summers she spends in South Carolina.

"Thank you for the popcorn," Pierre says, putting the bowl on her lap.

"I saw Ike at the library but your grandfather chased him away."

"Ike's so stupid. He's just frontin' with all that macho stuff like all the other boys."

"How you know?" asks Pierre, with popcorn in her mouth.

"Trust me," Jilline says, "I know boys and I know men. They don't know how to express themselves so they hide it under all this yeah-I'm-big-and-bad attitude. I've seen mad shows on TV on that subject. Oprah just did a show on it the other day. Can you stay long?" she asks me.

"My mother's not home," I tell her, "so I can stay a little longer."

"Good."

We look at each other for a while, not knowing what else to say. I want to talk with Jilline about Santos but I can't with Pierre there.

Jilline puts a tape in the VCR.

"Jilline," I start to say, "we don't have time to watch—" What I see on the TV stops me: two naked women and a man doing it.

"Oh, my God," Pierre says over and over.

"Remember that tape we found in the junkyard?" Jilline starts laughing and pointing at the TV. I had forgotten all about it.

"Lookit him go!" Jilline says.

Even Pierre is giggling. I don't think it's funny at all. One woman looks like she's in pain and all three are cursing at each other.

"H-he's raping her," I finally say.

"No, he's not, Mardi," says Jilline, rolling her eyes. "Sometimes people like a little pain. This is like coffee without milk and sugar: nasty!"

I look from the TV to Jilline, to Pierre, to my feet. What should I be thinking now? Should I be liking this? I keep imagining my mother and grandmother in the room staring at me. What would I say to them if they knew what I'm seeing? Why do I let things happen to me?

"Turn it off, Jilline," I say. Now the woman on the tape sounds like a goat getting killed for someone's dinner.

"Why?" Jilline asks.

"Because I said *no!*" I scream at her. "Because I don't want to watch your stupid movie! Because I don't want to be here anymore!" I stand up. Pierre's eyes are glued to the TV.

"Then get out my house then!" Jilline yells back, also standing up. "Don't come in here yelling at me!"

"Ale-ou vouzan!" I curse back at her in Créole. "If that's what you want!" I pull Pierre up by the arm. The bowl of popcorn falls off her lap and all over the carpet. But when I turn to leave, I come face to face with Jilline's grandfather.

"My class was canceled," is all he says, looking from the TV to me to Jilline.

"Granddaddy!" Jilline runs to turn the VCR off but must have pushed the fast-forward button.

I grab Pierre and run out the door.

I don't see Jilline at school for the next few days. I know her grandfather would never beat her, but I want to know what's going to happen to me. I don't want to call her. Mr. Hunter either unplugs the phone or answers it himself when he punishes Jilline. He hasn't called my house or Pierre's to tell on us. At least not yet.

I'm too scared to think of what will happen to me when he does call. My mother would definitely use her favorite leather belt on me, but I'm more worried about afterward, how they would treat me. Maman, Papa, and Grandmère would think I'm a dirty girl. And once they think that, I wouldn't have a chance at anything.

I'm the princess of angels waiting for Mr. Hunter to call. I laugh at all my father's jokes, good or bad, speak French with my grandmother—she likes that—and even give Serina five dollars and force a smile with Uncle Perrin.

To impress my mother, I clean the bathroom, the kitchen, our bedroom, and the living room. I dust, wipe, polish, mop, vacuum, and scrub everything I can. Grandmère thinks I'm sick with some kind of strange fever.

I freeze every time the phone rings. Serina sees this. "You've done something wrong, haven't you?" she asks.

"N-no," I say as calmly as I can.

"You're lying. Why all of a sudden are you cleaning like a chicken that's lost its head?"

"Okay," I whisper. I have to tell her something. "Don't tell Maman, but I saw the portable CD player I want for Christmas." That seems to satisfy her and she leaves me alone.

My father is in the middle of telling us a *blag* when Jilline finally calls me. My father continues his joke while I go into the bathroom for privacy.

Pélé is playing with his rubber ducky at the sink. He's splashing water all over the floor and singing "Row Your Boat."

"Could you please leave?" I ask sweetly. "I need to use the phone."

"Go to hell!" Pélé says in English, pressing each word. "I play here! Now!" And he continues singing a Créole version of "Crow Yo Bow." I want to take him by his little ears and shake him but I step inside the bathtub, pull the curtains, and make myself into a ball at one end. You'd think there's a madman in the house and I'm trying to call for help.

"Wh-what happened?" I whisper into the phone.

"I've been in prison!" Jilline says.

"Come on, Jilline! Dunt–*don't*–play like that!"

"Okay, okay, calm down. I can't go anywhere but school for the next month and I'm only allowed to watch channel thirteen."

"That's it?"

"Yes, Mardi, that is prison."

"Well," I gulp, "what about me?"

"Nothing's gonna happen to you, I don't think."

"How do you know?"

"Because my granddaddy says he talked to your uncle, and your uncle said–"

"What! Your grandfather talked to Uncle Perrin?"

"Yeah. That's what Granddaddy says."

"But my uncle doesn't speak English."

"Looks like he knew enough English to know what went down. Your uncle even gave Granddaddy advice on what to do and not to do to punish me. I don't know why you don't like him. I got one month instead of two months in prison because of him. Thank him for me."

"Did your grandfather talk to anyone else?"

"Granddaddy said he thought more about it later and he knows if he told on you, your parents would probably blindfold and shoot you."

"So he's not going to call back?"

"No, he's not. I don't even think he'll call Pierre's father. But he says he wants to talk to you and Pierre like he talked to me."

"Jilline?"

"Yeah?"

"Why didn't you come to school, then?"

"I made myself sick. After eating I'd make myself throw up. I threw up in the kitchen and in Granddaddy's bedroom, hoping he'd have some pity on me, you know? It stopped working after a while."

"Well, okay . . . I have to go now. Thanks for calling."

"Sure."

For the next few days I watch Uncle Perrin and try to be wherever he is. I keep a list of who he talks to in the house and what about. So far he hasn't given any sign that he knows. I polish his guitar and when I hand it back to him, he just smiles and thanks me. He treats me the same, being polite and all but nothing else.

I want to believe that maybe he doesn't know anything. He's had plenty of times to say something. Like last night Maman was saying that our neighbor down the hall has a fifteen-year-old daughter who's pregnant for the second time.

"See?" my mother said. "Kids today know too much."

"Aaahhh, and they don't know what to do with all that knowledge!" Grandmère added.

"Me? I would shoot any boy who touched my daughters," said my father. "Polette, could you imagine in my day and time to be coming up to your father, getting you pregnant, and walking away?"

"My father?" said my mother. "Maybe if you found him sober he would try to kill you for it." Maman was raised by her father. When he got drunk, which was almost all the time, he would try to break everything he owned, including my mother.

"Aaahhh, these young men know that now when they plant their seeds in the garden there's no gardener to chase them away," said Grandmère.

Uncle Perrin saw me near the kitchen listening but he didn't say anything.

Why?

What's he waiting for?

Tonight Uncle Perrin is hand washing his shirt and socks in a bucket in the bathtub. Pélé is already asleep, so my uncle is alone.

I knock on the bathroom door, even though it's halfway open.

"Hello, Uncle. Is it okay if I brush my teeth?"

"Come in, Biskwit," he says.

I still hate it when he calls me that, but I pretend I like it. I take my toothbrush, inspect it, feel its bristles, take the toothpaste, unscrew the top, and squeeze from the end of the tube. I even floss. I once heard Uncle Perrin saying he wanted to be a dentist when he was a boy.

I watch him while I do everything. But Uncle Perrin doesn't notice. He's too busy trying to wash his socks.

Please, Uncle, say something.

"If I listen to these black socks," he finally says, "I'll rinse them until they're white again."

I laugh. Uncle Perrin looks up at me as if I just told him I'd seen the Virgin Mary. Then he starts laughing, too. But when he sees me laughing too hard, he stops.

"What's with you, Mardi?" he asks. "It wasn't that funny."

"Yes, it was," I say, trying to keep the act up. "You're a very funny man!"

"Mardi!" I hear my mother say from her bedroom. "Why aren't you in bed?"

"She's with me," Uncle Perrin answers her. "I know what you're doing, Mardi," he continues, lowering his voice, "and it won't work. I spoke with your little friend's father already."

"He's her grandfather," I say, dropping my act completely. At least now it's over.

"He said you and Pierre were watching—"

"Where'd you learn to speak English, Uncle?"

"At the English Institute in Haiti, and don't change the subject."

"It wasn't my fault! It wasn't my tape! I didn't know Jilline was going to watch it! I just went to her house and she put it in the VCR! I told her I didn't want to watch it—"

"I believe you."

"—and when I got up to leave that's when her grandfather came. . . ."

"I said I believe you, Mardi."

"Huh?"

"Do you have wax in your ears?"

"Huh?"

Uncle Perrin laughs. "I remember I got caught like that when I was young with a drawing someone made. One of the older boys at school hid the drawing in my book bag and when I got home your grandmother opened my bag, and well . . ." He shows me a half-moon-shaped mark on his shoulder. "Let's say I still have memories of it and I don't want you to have memories of something that is not your fault."

"Huh?" I say again.

"Mardi," he says, "go to bed. I won't tell, but don't let anyone call here with that kind of news again."

"Yes, Uncle," I say. "Good night."

"Bonne nuit," he says.

Tonight I sleep a little easier. I lie in bed taking deep breaths, trying not to move too much with the rocks in my bed. Even though he won't tell, we still won't be friends. It's still his fault I'm in this country, anyhow, because he didn't want to shut up about things.

"Shut up. . . ." I can teach him about those two words. I know how to keep quiet so everyone thinks you're dead.

I take deep breaths and roll over so that I'm facing the cracked wall. I think about the half-moon-shaped mark on Uncle Perrin's shoulder. Did Grandmère really do that to him? Did she let him explain that it wasn't his drawing?

"Mardi! Mardi, are you asleep?"

Aunt Widza.

"No, I'm here," I answer. "Go to bed, Matant." I feel her cold hands grab my arm. I don't turn around.

"Please, Mardi," she whispers. "You're the only one who can help me!"

"What is it now?" I ask.

"Every time we turn out the lights I see all the *bakas* coming out of the closet and under the bed."

"You had a bad dream."

"No, Mardi!"

"Shhhh. Lower your voice."

"Everyone thinks I'm crazy. I'm not. I'm just scared of those demons under the bed and in those closets."

I move closer to the wall and pull my comforter back to make a place for her. She climbs up into my bed.

"Thank you, Mardi. Your bed is bumpy but I feel all right. You're the only one who listens to me. Do you know your importance?" She kisses my forehead, then closes her eyes and puts one arm behind her neck. I slowly move my head until I'm resting on her shoulder.

"Matant?" I whisper.

"Yes," she whispers back, eyes still closed.

"How's work?"

"Good, thank you. I have a lot of friends who stop by to talk to me. But they rarely buy anything and Mr. Amorez doesn't like that."

"What kind of friends do you have?"

"The kind that always gives me compliments. I'll play with them sometimes but I'm so much smarter than they think. *Bonne nuit,* Mardi."

"Good night, Matant." But I lie awake another hour wondering what she meant.

My grandmother used to wake up before the cock crowed. Here in Flatbush Grandmère Adda sleeps tight and gets up late every day. But I saw her very early this morning sitting by herself in the kitchen. I was on my way to the bathroom when I heard shuffling. I tiptoed closer. The lights were turned off but I could see her, clearly lit by the candle on the table. She was flipping through what looked like a photo album, caressing the edges of every page. At one point she stopped and looked up right at me, but I backed away and she returned to her book.

Now she is humming and cooking in the kitchen. I'm about to leave for school when she calls me in to eat with Pélé. She's fried eggs and herring and boiled baby green plantains. She's even baked the bread herself and made us papaya shakes. Pélé is finishing his second plate while I'm halfway through my first. I watch her open and close cupboards, tasting, chopping, seasoning; hair tangled, robe inside out. And then she sings out loud the song she's been humming: "What Can I Do to Make You Happy?" I sing the last lines of it, too.

"You still remember that song?" she says.

"Papa liked to sing it to you," I answer. "A long time ago they came and surprised you. It was your birthday. Papa sang you that song and Maman gave you a yellow dress—"

"No, it was cream—"

"—with flowers on it and Uncle Perrin gave you this vase with—"

"—glass flowers." Grandmère is laughing: tiny teeth and wrinkles. "Aaahhh, Mardi. I dreamt about two people I love."

"Me?"

"You? Aaahhh, your footprints are all over my dreams. Last night my husband and my mother came back to me. I rarely dream about them but . . . they were both there together, fresh and healthy. Good things happen whenever I see them. *Un bèl rèv!* A beautiful dream!"

"Grandmère, are you happy here?"

"Aaahhh, Mardi. I am the master of nothing here. But what can I do? If my country was in order I would be the first one to return. You and Serina are the lucky ones. You're both young and can change, especially you, Mardi, maybe because you were born here. You're the American. You're born with choices."

"I wish I had your dreams, Grandmère."

"You don't want an old woman's dreams."

"I do."

"You're just a baby. All you need to do is choose your life. Mine is ending. My country is in one place and I'm in another. I wish you could lend me some of your dreams."

"I wouldn't do that to you."

"Are you being stingy or don't you have good dreams anymore?"

Instead of answering her, I look at Pélé. He glances down at his clean plate and licks off his frosty papaya mustache. He presses his lips together and slides an orange building block across the table to me. I zip it in my book bag.

As Grandmère bends to take more bread out of the oven, I touch her back. I think I can feel her heartbeat, but maybe it's just the heavy ticking of my Mickey Mouse watch.

Should I close my eyes and sip the warm school milk as if I like it? Or should I make believe I am working on a math problem that is so hard, I have no time to look up and notice Santos two tables away from me in the lunchroom? He's by himself again, staring at me, and this is the second week in a row he's done this. He'll stay for about five minutes and then leave.

Is this the way love starts? By staring and making the other person feel like they're sitting on ice?

I like it.

No I don't.

Yes I do.

No.

Well, maybe a little.

But I know I'm not supposed to. What reason does Maman give for this one? I think she said boys won't respect you if they know you like them. But why would they stay around if you act like you don't like them?

It feels so good! I like the way he's looking at me! I don't feel like I should be hiding myself. I mean, he doesn't make me feel dirty, like it's my fault he's watching me.

I don't know. It's all mashed potatoes in my head.

I look at my watch. It's been five minutes.

Okay, here it comes: the wink. Santos winks at me and I feel it like he's just thrown a rock made of feathers at me: hard at first, but then in the middle you find something sweet, like sucking on a sugarcane.

I wish I were Serina. She would know how to act.

Then he comes and sits right across from me.

What I think?

I think I'm going to explode all over him!

"So how you doin'?" he asks me, nodding like we've been talking all along.

I can't answer him.

"What's up? You can't talk?" he asks, this time smiling.

I smile back, lower my eyes and nod.

"Then say something," he says.

"H-hello."

He laughs. "You Haitian, right?"

Oh, God, no! He knows! I want to die!

"Say something in Créole, then," he says.

The words fly out of my mouth before I can stop them: *"Mwen ta vle-ou renmin mwen menm si mwen pa bèl, menm si mwen pa pròp."*

"What does that mean?" he asks, amazed.

I would like you to like me even though I'm not pretty and I'm not clean. But I don't tell him what I really said. "It—it's just words t-to a song about a girl that lost her cheeken—*chicken*." I feel so stupid.

Santos laughs. "So what you doing after school?"

"Home." I shrug.

"You wanna come play with me at my house?"

Now I'm the one looking amazed.

"Just video games." He spoons some of my mashed potatoes and throws it on the wall. It sticks there like a ball of glue.

"I—I have to go home."

"Oh, it's like that, huh? You do everything people tell you, right? You one of those good girls, huh?"

If only he knew.

"I seen your aunt in my father's store."

"She, my aunt, sh-she a little . . . crazy." I have to tell him *something*.

"Yeah, crazy is good. I like crazy. You a little crazy, Mardi?"

This is the first time he's ever said my name. I shake my head. I'm not like my aunt and I never want to be.

"Maybe you are and just don't know it," he says, as if

he can see what I'm thinking. "You live by Newkirk, right?"

I nod.

"Yeah? Yeah?" he keeps saying, and I keep nodding until he hits me with: "Listen, you wanna go out?"

My eyes almost pop out of my head. Santos laughs again. "You're funny," he says. "You going to the Christmas dance at St. Joseph's next Saturday?"

I nod. What could keep me away? I went last year with Serina.

"Good," he says, and without saying good-bye he gets up. He has a white check mark on the front of his navy blue jogging suit. As he walks away, I see he also has check marks on the back of his squeaky sneakers. Santos always wears clothes with this mark on them. A lot of kids do. In Haiti we got a check in school only when we did something right; here you can buy and wear it.

I see Santos long after he leaves the cafeteria. I'm going to remember this day forever.

Later, in English class, I can't stop smiling and staring at the back of Santos's head. He asked me out. Santos asked me out! Hey, Santos asked me out! The Mildred Rodriguez is his girlfriend but Santos asked *me* out!

"Who would like to recite the poem on page one twenty-three?" Mrs. Orlando asks.

Now, there's two reasons why my arm shoots up: Ike and The Mildred Rodriguez are both absent today.

"Mardi? Great! Come on up."

I get up and stand in front of the class in my pink sweater and gray overalls. I close my eyes and breathe.

When I open them again, I only see Santos sitting in front of me and I'm in my red ballroom dress again. I don't need my textbook; I've memorized this:

"How do I love thee?
Let me count the ways. . . ."

When I finish, I close my eyes, and when I open them again, the whole class is back. Some roll their eyes, others giggle, but they all look at me like my head's in the wrong place.

"Wow, Mardi," says Mrs. Orlando. "Thank you. I think that's one of the most passionate renditions I've ever heard. Ms. Elizabeth Barrett Browning would have been proud."

I head back to my seat. As I pass Santos, he nods at me. When I get to my desk, I write in Malice: *I'm melting! Joy!* Later, when Mrs. Orlando steps out of the room, Jilline asks me, "What's wrong with you? You all happy and whatnot."

Should I tell her right now? Oh, why not?

"Really?" Jilline is surprised. "Oh, wow. I didn't think he'd ever say anything to you. Well, maybe he's just messing with you. Trust me, it's nothing serious."

"How do you know?"

"You know how boys are. You can't trust them. Even my granddaddy says so. And anyhow, Mildred is Santos's girl and she's real pretty and you know boys never leave pretty girls for . . ."

"For girls like me?"

"No, that's not what I was going to say. You so sensitive."

"Didn't you say Mildred Rodriguez wasn't so pretty? You said she was a dog!"

"Mardi, dag, calm down. You know I was only kidding to make you feel better."

I don't understand Jilline. It's only when I really want her to be happy for me that she's not.

"And also," Jilline continues, "your mother and father would kill you if they knew you were messing with boys."

"But I'm not the one who did anything."

"It doesn't matter what you did or didn't do. You know how your family is." I think I see Jilline smiling to herself when she says this, as if she's glad that I'm not so happy anymore.

The moment in the cafeteria I said would last forever starts to fade because in my mind, right after Santos says "You wanna go out?" I see myself sitting in a chair with my mother, father, and grandmother standing in front of me, demanding to know who this Santos boy is and from where and how well do I know him. I don't know how to answer them.

The bell wakes me up. I look down at my hand. I've dug a small hole in the center of my palm with my pen.

I walk home from school happy with nervous and sad swimming inside me. The school nurse wrapped up my hand pretty good. It doesn't even hurt. I'll tell everyone that I was playing with my pen and accidentally stabbed myself.

I keep thinking about Santos and "You wanna go out?" over and over. Imagine me on a date with Santos. . . .

But here is Ike, standing in an alley.

"Leave me alone," I whisper.

"You say something, island girl?"

"Leave me alone," I say, louder.

Ike's head moves back like I've pushed him. I'm surprised, too, so I say it again: "Leave me alone!"

Ike laughs and when I see his teeth, I want to kneel down in front of him and beg him to have mercy. "So Mardi ain't gonna let me push her around?" He grabs me by my shoulder and shoves me against a metal streetlight post.

"Why you letting that Dominican boy talk to you?" he says. He is less than an inch from my face. "You don't know him like I do."

I don't look him in the eye.

"Look at me!" he says. "Look at me!"

But today I'm too fast for him. I slip out of his trap and run.

When I get home, I smell paint.

I walk into the living room and see all the furniture on a little island in the middle of the room. Uncle Perrin and Aunt Widza are painting the room a baby yellow color. They seem to be the only ones home.

"What are you two doing?"

"We're painting," Uncle Perrin answers. He has on a short-sleeve shirt even though all the windows are wide open and it's freezing.

"And I'm covering the small places he missed," says Aunt Widza. Her fingertips are covered in paint. "That is different from painting. Do you want to help?"

"Go wash your hand," I tell her. I start closing all the windows.

"Don't, Mardi," Uncle Perrin says. "The smell of the paint will be too strong." He reopens the windows halfway. Then he sees my face. "What happened to your—"

"I fell," I tell him, and I'm not lying. I slipped when I ran from Ike.

"You fall a lot, don't you?" he asks.

"Mardi is a clever child," says Aunt Widza. "You punch her on the right and she turns and punches herself on the left just to trick you into thinking you've hit her twice."

"Who told you you could paint the house?" I continue shutting the windows.

"I told your father the first day I got here that the color of these walls is too depressing," he says. "In Haiti, it would be fine to paint your walls a dark color because you can always look out the window to the sunshine. Here you have so many days that aren't sunny."

"The sun doesn't have to shine every day," I say. "Happiness isn't a color and it doesn't last!"

"True," he says, rolling another coat of paint on the wall. "But I've got the time to do the work now, so I got the paint from the super. What I'm doing won't hurt anyone."

"How do you know you're not hurting anyone if you never stop to look or ask?"

He puts his brush down. "I asked your father."

"My father lives here with four other people—"

"You forgot me," Aunt Widza says. "I'm number five."

"I wasn't talking to you! Look at you! I hear you're being very nice to men at the supermarket!"

Uncle Perrin gives Aunt Widza a questioning look.

"The other day I went to the bathroom," she says. "I was in a hurry and didn't realize afterward that I hadn't pulled my skirt all the way down. Yes, there was a show, but I hadn't planned it and when I realized why people were staring at me I ended it."

"Widza," says Uncle Perrin, "what I understand from Henri is that he didn't even want you working at all. If there is going to be some kind of problem in the future—"

"I am not a child, and I am not a whore. When I smile at someone it's because I'm happy, not because I want to sex them!"

"Widza!"

"And," Aunt Widza continues, "I'm pretty. I attract attention. Some of us have that gift, Mardi, and no matter how hard we try nothing can hide it."

We stay quiet for a long moment, feeding off each other's thoughts. I look from Uncle Perrin to Aunt Widza, Uncle Perrin looks from me to her, but Aunt Widza stares straight ahead at the front door, like someone she's trying to recognize is standing there.

The phone rings.

"This must be them," Uncle Perrin says to Aunt Widza.

He goes to the kitchen. Aunt Widza's gaze falls on me. She takes a few steps toward me and stops. Her eyes have something in them that I don't understand. She's not angry, she's not happy, she's . . . calm.

"Hello? . . . Yes, this is Perrin. . . . Yeah . . . Uh-huh . . . Oh? Good! . . . So Pélé will be staying with you? . . . We'll miss him. . . . He likes it, huh? . . . Okay, I'll see you all tomorrow." He hangs up and rushes over to Aunt Widza. "It looks like they're keeping him."

"Saint Joseph! We've found his family!" says Aunt Widza. They do a little dance, completely ignoring me.

"Where is Pélé?" I finally ask. They stop dancing and get back to painting.

"Your wish came true," Uncle Perrin says, picking up his brush. "We found Pélé's family."

"What do you mean?" I ask. "He's not here anymore? But he was here this morning. I saw him."

"Don't worry, Mardi," says Uncle Perrin. "We'll go see him from time to time. He's only in Queens. We found out Pélé's mother has an aunt there who's been searching for him and his mother. We took him to her this morning."

"And you're letting Pélé stay with these people just like that?" I ask. "You don't know them. What if they're kidnappers?" I don't know why I'm not jumping for joy. This is what I wanted, right?

"Pélé's mother showed me a picture of her and her aunt, and her aunt had the same picture on her wall. It was amazing. This aunt had visited Pélé and his mother in Haiti a few years ago. Don't worry, Mardi. We won't lose touch with him. Pélé needs to know we're not far. None of this is easy for him, but it's good he's finally with his family. Immigration and children's social services know everything."

"I already miss him, too," says Aunt Widza.

"He was such a good companion, that child," Uncle Perrin says. "When we were in the camps in Cuba, he was always happy and trying to make other people laugh until his mother died."

"He must have seen a lot," says Aunt Widza. "From the schoolyard to the refugee camp yard, from taking a bath in a basin to taking a bath in a sea full of sharks. They suffer so young, these children. And when they get old they're as hard as wood."

"Yes," says Uncle Perrin. He paints for a moment. "But we'll call and visit him. He hasn't lost us, and I made sure he understands that."

I stand by and watch the two of them talking and painting like a husband and wife, or, better yet, like the brother and sister they are. All this time Pélé and Uncle Perrin have been with us, not once did I think about what they had to go through to get here. We all had to do something, give up something to get here. I should have tried to understand Pélé; he was only a little boy. I hope he won't still be sleeping in a bathtub.

I notice the muscles on Uncle Perrin's shoulders tightening and loosening like a thick rubber band with every stroke of his roller. I remember him being very skinny in Haiti, like I'm skinny now.

"Why didn't you ask me what color paint I wanted?" I interrupt their conversation. "I don't like that color."

"Yellow is a good choice," Aunt Widza says. "Yellow is for good luck and New Year's and pineapples. And besides, I don't care what you like."

I storm past her, telling her under my breath, "Shut up."

"What did you say?" Uncle Perrin stops painting.

I face him. "Nothing. I didn't say anything and I didn't do anything."

"Mardi," Uncle Perrin says, putting the roller down. He walks toward me, stopping a few feet away. I look at Aunt Widza. She has her fingers in her mouth.

"Mardi!" he says again sharply. "*Dit mwen.* Tell me. What is going on with you? I can understand when a child is occasionally fresh, but you are always mean-faced when it comes to me and your aunt."

"We are in her space," Aunt Widza says. "My niece has always hated me." She turns away and gently knocks her forehead against the wall. When she faces us again, she has a yellow spot in the middle of her forehead, and she looks as sad as a puppy.

I hold back a smile by looking at my feet. "Oh, I don't hate you, Matant." Uncle Perrin sighs loudly and steps closer to me.

I still look down. Uncle Perrin has no shoes on. His feet look like a truck rolled over them. His toenails are busted and cracked; the bunions make it look like he has fifteen toes instead of ten. He places his hand on my shoulder. I want to move back but something keeps me there. His hands are firm and warm. I can feel them even through my sweater.

This is strange. I almost want to rest my head on his chest. Maybe he will understand. He likes to help people, my uncle. He'll get into trouble for people.

But I'm supposed to be hating him.

"Mardi," he says. "Mardi, you don't remember this. You don't remember when you used to follow me wherever I went. I was your father and the big brother you never had. You don't remember that when you had food you would share it with me first. You forget how you used to say you would marry me when you grew up, and how you'd build a big house by the L'Artibonite River for us to live in."

"I was a nice girl then," I answer.

He nods and lets me go. I turn around and head to the bedroom. As I pass the front door, I see a new picture taped there, a picture of a younger-looking Pélé, a young woman that must be his mother, and an older woman, maybe that aunt in Queens. A family reunited. Uncle Perrin's accomplishment.

Some nights I go to bed with my father's flashlight.
I shine the light on the cracks in the ceiling and make up
stories of what they really could be and how they got there.
Some are shaped like small islands, and I can see Cuba,
Jamaica, Puerto Rico. And on a good night, I can even see
all of Hispaniola. That's what Haiti and the Dominican
Republic were called long ago.

Hispaniola.

MardiSantos.

SantosMardi.

Sometimes I think there's a big friendly magic dragon
like Puff who lives upstairs and practices the waltz while
everyone is sleeping. That's how the cracks get there. Each
step the dragon takes makes a new island.

I hear Uncle Perrin in the living room softly playing his
guitar. He's got the sofa all to himself now. He listens to

this classical music station on the radio and plays along, copying at first, then adding his own notes. He's getting really good. I wish he would play the "Flower Duet" song from my blue purse. I could listen to that forever. We study classical music in my music appreciation class at school, but most kids can't stand it. I don't think it's that bad. You have to be in the mood for it; you have to learn to stay real still so you can hear it. It's the kind of music you think you can hear when it's not being played.

I heard it in my grandmother's backyard in Port-au-Prince when I saw two butterflies kissing and dancing. I tried to catch them, to put them in a box and take them in the house, but they knew better and flew high and away.

I close my eyes and two seconds later someone grabs the flashlight from my hand.

"Go to sleep, Mardi!" says Serina. She gets back into her bed thinking she's actually done something to help me fall asleep.

I'm running through my grandmother's backyard, but the yard is a cemetery. The tombstones have pictures of my family on them. They wave good-bye to me as I fly past them. The leaves and branches from the cha cha trees whip my back. I feel fingertips, hands trying to grab me by the neck. I turn around and see Uncle Perrin and Aunt Widza running after me, trying to stop me.

I know them.

But I can't stop and I jump over a cliff, into a violet-red sky, into a . . .

$\bullet \quad \bullet \quad \bullet$

My face is cold.

Someone is shaking me awake.

Before opening my eyes I strike out and hit something—someone. When I do open them, I find myself on the bathroom floor with my mother, who is shocked, holding the side of her face. I don't know how I got here. A pair of scissors is in one hand and my other hand is holding myself between my legs. I quickly move that hand away and pull my nightgown down over my thighs.

"What's wrong with you?" my mother gasps. "Something better be wrong with you for hitting me like that!"

I look around the bathroom. Everyone is there: Papa, Grandmère, Aunt Widza, Serina, and Uncle Perrin.

"Aaahhh, I came into the bathroom to pee and I saw her lying there," Grandmère says.

My father helps me off the floor and onto the toilet seat cover. The front of my nightgown is cut. The front of my thigh is hurting. I try to cover it, not knowing what I've done to myself.

"Why did you do this?" my father asks, taking the scissors away from me.

"I—I don't know."

"What do you mean you don't know?" asks my mother.

"I—I was trying to make my nightgown shorter."

"I don't know what to do with you," my mother says. "You wake up in the middle of the night to go play in the bathroom and scare your grandmother to death. Mardi, what's the matter with you?"

"I—I wasn't feeling well," I say, keeping my eyes on the floor, not wanting anybody to see what's inside them.

My father feels my head. "Maybe she's sick," he says.

"Yes, Mardi is sick," says Aunt Widza. "I've seen her go into the bathroom late at night and not come out until morning. I hear her moving around like she's playing tag with herself."

"You crazy liar!" I say.

My mother grabs my arm. "Widza is your aunt, she's old enough to be your mother! Where do you come from, talking to her that way?" She shakes me and does not let go. *"Dit pardon!"*

I look to my father for help, but he says, "You shouldn't disrespect your aunt."

"It's okay," says Aunt Widza. "Mardi didn't mean it. Polette, you can let go."

"No!" my mother says. "First she plays around at night in the bathroom, then she wants to hit and call people liars. What's next? Soon she'll want to call the police on us for child abuse like Clara Metro's daughter did to her, remember that? The girl was fifteen and coming in at two o'clock in the morning every night. When Clara whipped her she had the nerve to call the police. You see, Mardi behaved when she was back in Haiti, she knew her place as a child and that's what she still is and if she's forgotten I'll beat it back into her! I don't care if the police come get me. When I was her age I had two jobs and skin thick enough to take my own father's beatings. Does this child think I have the time to play with children?"

Instead of crying, I hold my breath. I think of all the mothers I want instead of her.

No one says anything. No one does anything to help me, either. They all stand there watching her pinch a hole in my arm and go on and on about her stupid little hard childhood with a drunk grandfather I never knew.

I close my eyes and after I count to three, I'm going to scream.

One . . . two . . . three . . .

"Okay, Polette," Uncle Perrin says.

I feel his hands unhooking my mother's grip.

"She has not said—"

"It's all right," Uncle Perrin says, freeing my arm.

I breathe out and open my eyes.

"You're lucky your uncle's here," my mother says, glaring, rubbing the side of her face where I hit her. One by one everyone leaves except Uncle Perrin and Aunt Widza.

"I'm sorry, Mardi," says Aunt Widza. She walks out of the bathroom, leaving me alone with Uncle Perrin. He stands there for what seems like a long time. I look at the floor, picking dust balls from the furry toilet seat cover. When he still doesn't say anything, I pat the new scar on my thigh.

Then Uncle Perrin sighs loudly. "I'd like to walk you to school today."

I nod.

Uncle Perrin and I walk the first four blocks without saying a word. The December wind is cold. I fix my knapsack on my back and cross my arms in front of my chest for more protection. I notice Uncle Perrin has on a pair of green socks with open-toed summer shoes.

"Your feet aren't cold?" I ask.

"I'm okay," he answers, rubbing his hands together. He doesn't have gloves on either.

"Why didn't you borrow Papa's boots?" I ask.

"I'm tired of asking him for things," he says.

"But you need them."

"True, but . . . I'm also tired of depending on other people. I'll be moving out soon as I can get a good job."

We walk another block in silence.

"I'm sorry I was mean to you," I say. "I didn't like you—I hated you—when you first came."

"Why?"

"Because . . . because I thought that if you hadn't gotten into trouble in Haiti, we all wouldn't be here."

"What do you mean?" He stops walking.

I face him, not sure if I should be telling him what I'm about to tell him. "When the coup d'état happened in Haiti, a lot of bad things happened to people, to girls, too."

"Did anything happen to you, Mardi?" He leans forward, looking me straight in the eye.

I lower my eyes and point to my knee. "I fell and cut myself," I say, and it isn't a lie. It isn't a complete truth, either.

He seems satisfied with my answer and nods for me to go on.

"Well, when the coup happened, people were getting killed and a lot of bad things happened to people—to girls, too, and Philippe, Cousin Philippe.... You know they dumped his body in front of our house, and Philippe, he was only fifteen, and so when you wouldn't stop talking, and the people killing people—and girls, too—when those people came by the house to look for you and when you weren't there, they killed Philippe and the maid's son and so that's why me and Serina and everyone else had to leave and come here, because you wouldn't stop talking."

There.

It's out. Some of it. I take a deep breath. It's the longest sentence I've ever said in my life. I expect my uncle to get angry but he doesn't say anything. He nods for me to continue.

"And sometimes I don't like it here," I say. "Sometimes I want to go back to Haiti, but I can't."

The radio said this morning the windchill factor is eight degrees, but right now I'm not feeling as cold as I did a minute ago. The wind blows the ends of my scarf around my head. But I feel warm, like a small fire is starting under my feet.

"Kids make fun of me," I continue. "I don't hurt them but they want to hurt me, and I don't know how to make them stop and I don't know why Maman and Papa don't hear me. They think paying bills and giving me food is more important. And when I speak up they say I'm fresh.

Everything's changed but everyone thinks they're still the same. But one day, you'll see, I'm not going to be . . ."

"Be what?" my uncle asks.

"Be . . . quiet," I answer, mostly to myself.

But Uncle Perrin hears me. "You're learning," he says. "You're learning more than you think you know. Now let's get you to school. I'm freezing!" He puts his arm around my shoulder, and as we walk, I lean on him, something I should have done a long time ago.

There are Christmas decorations everywhere and everyone looks happy, like something wonderful is about to happen, like they've never seen Christmas before. I get excited, too—the Christmas dance is in a few days.

Santos.

He doesn't come sit down at lunch anymore, but when I saw him once in the hallway, he nodded my way. The Mildred Rodriguez was with him at the time. She turned around and looked me up and down like something was rotting on me.

Santos hasn't been in school all week. Aunt Widza told Papa that Santos's mother is having problems with her lungs and is sick in the hospital again. I hope his mother gets better and that Santos isn't too sad to go to the dance.

Ike.

As I walk up the stairs to history class, I slow my steps.

I'm alone with him in history—no Santos or Jilline. But he sits all the way up front on one side and I'm in the back on the other. He hardly shows up for class, so he doesn't have much of a chance to get in my way.

If Ike would disappear, I'd be happy for the rest of my life. But, I must say, Ike's been good to me lately. I don't know what's wrong with him. Maybe it's because I finally told him to leave me alone when he caught me on the street. Maybe he thinks I'm not afraid of him anymore. In class he stares at me and doesn't say anything. And yesterday, Ike surprised everyone.

"Can anyone tell me what the *Amistad* was?" the teacher asked. Ms. Pine was a substitute and was just as afraid of Ike as the rest of the class. No one was paying attention to her except me, so Ms. Pine asked the question again. This time a little louder.

"Slave ship," a voice answered. Ms. Pine looked around the room, trying to figure out who it was.

"I said the damn *Amistad* was a slave ship!" Ike said. His head had been on the desk and he raised it and sat up. His voice was angry, but it sounded like he had been crying. I had seen his eyes when I first walked into class. They were wet and red. For a moment I wanted to be sorry for him, but I caught myself.

Ms. Pine jumped when she realized it was Ike who had spoken.

"Yeah," Ike continued. "They was taking all these slaves from, from Africa to New York, see, so they could work for free in those factories, but those slaves were slick and said 'nah-uh' and they bum-rushed the captain and turned that boat around ... or did they go to New York anyway and burn the factories?"

The room was so quiet we could hear Ike thinking: it sounded like paper ripping.

After about a minute of staring at Ike, Ms. Pine finally said, "Well, uh, Isaac, you've got the right idea, except the ship was going from one part of Cuba to another."

"I don't know what they did after that," Ike said, ignoring Ms. Pine. "I really don't know what they did after. . . . Do you, Mardi?"

Everyone turned and looked at me. The only answer I had was to look down and be silent.

Ike.

He lowered his head back onto the desk and went to sleep.

No one bothered to wake him up when the bell rang.

When I get home from school, I smell food frying the second I open the front door. It's sweet and spicy and it almost makes me hungry, except I ate a bag of potato chips and three packs of Boston Baked Beans candy on my way here. I go to the kitchen and find my uncle ducking from the grease popping out of the *griyo* he's frying. He looks as if he's in a boxing match with the pork, trying not to get hit.

"Bonjour, Monnonk," I say, smiling.

"Good afternoon, Mardi," he says in English. "How your school was doing today?"

"It's 'How was school today,' " I laugh, correcting him.

"You are the expert," he says. A grease ball hits him in the face. He jumps back, rubbing his right cheek.

"It got you?" I ask. "Do you want me to get some ice?"

"No." He shakes his head and returns to the stove.

"Where's Matant Widza?"

"At work."

I look over all the food my uncle is preparing: sweet and green fried plantains, fried sweet potatoes, *pikliz* (spiced hot relish), green salad, potato salad, rice with *djondjon,* and *labapen. Labapen* is this small jackfruit that tastes like bitter boiled potatoes. It is one of my favorite things to eat, and I haven't seen one since I left Haiti.

"Where'd you get the *labapen?*" I take one from the bowl and smell it.

"Anne."

"Who's Anne?"

"Madan Novembre, eh, Patrick's mother?"

"Oh?"

"Yes. A friend of hers just came from Haiti and gave her a lot of things. Anne, eh, Madan Novembre also gave me a bag of dried mushrooms–that's why we're eating rice with *djondjon* today. And she gave me *pitimi, ble, chanmchanm,* and even *kakaro* so we can make real hot chocolate."

"Really? That was very nice of her."

"Yeah."

I squeeze the *labapen,* mushing it in my hand.

"You are going to eat your dinner right now, my nephew?" Uncle practices his English.

"No, not right now," I say, throwing the *labapen* in the

garbage behind his back. "And I'm your niece, not your nephew."

"Okay." He winks. "You are the expert."

I take a can of soda from the refrigerator, leaving him to fight the pork.

Later that night everyone is in the living room eating and complimenting Uncle Perrin's cooking. Uncle Perrin placed all the food on the living room table and set up napkins and plates like he was having a party and we were his guests.

"Hey," says Serina. "Remember Gracia? That old cook we had?"

"Aaahhh, how can I forget?" says Grandmère. "She used to want to argue with me in my house, in my own kitchen."

Aunt Widza, Serina, and I smile secretly at each other. Gracia was a cranky old woman who thought the kitchen was as holy as a church. For some reason she couldn't stand Serina and snitched to Grandmère about her every chance she had. Once she threw both me and Aunt Widza out of the kitchen when Aunt Widza was boiling milk to help me fall asleep. During the next week Gracia's false teeth would mysteriously disappear and reappear in weird places like the oven, hanging on a nail in the outhouse, and one time in a pitcher of lemonade.

"Gracia always wanted her table perfect," Uncle Perrin says.

"Like her teeth," giggles Aunt Widza.

"Yes," Serina says, "Donkey-Teeth Gracia."

I snort and neigh. Everyone laughs except Maman and Papa.

"How come I don't know this Gracia?" my mother asks.

"She came and left between one of your visits," says Grandmère.

"Was this the Gracia that lived by Saint Don Bosco Church?" asks my father.

"No, no," says Uncle Perrin. "You're thinking of someone else. This Gracia was from a faraway northern village near Cap-Haitien."

"Oh," Maman and Papa say together.

"Aaahhh, Perrin, you were one of the best cooks in the family," Grandmère says. "Just like your father."

"Daddy used to feed me," Aunt Widza says.

"Now, Widza," says my grandmother, "do you even remember your father?"

"Of course I do," Aunt Widza says. "I was six when he died, Perrin was nine, and Henri was twenty-seven. Daddy had on a blue suit, his favorite. His coffin was this ruby red color. Before they closed Daddy forever you ran up to him, took a silver butterfly barrette from your hair, and pinned it on his suit. You cried, 'Take this. I am one wing from this butterfly and you were the other. How will I fly now, missing you?' "

My father and uncle glance at her, then at each other. Grandmère's lips twitch, her hands tremble. She takes a deep breath and quickly finishes her food.

"Today was cold," Aunt Widza says after a while. "Saturday they say it will be better."

"That's good," Serina says. "I want to wear my new shoes for the dance on Saturday."

"What dance?" my mother asks.

"The Christmas dance at Saint Joseph's," I say. "We went last year, remember?"

"What time is this dance?" she asks Serina.

"It's from seven o'clock to midnight," I answer.

"Wait a minute," my father says, "wasn't there a gun-fight at the dance last year?"

"It was way after we had left, and it happened across the street from the church," Serina says.

"You went with them last year, Henri," Maman says. "Are you going?"

"No," Papa answers.

"Why not?" Serina and I cry together. We know that if Papa doesn't go, we won't go.

"Clara Metro invited us to a party at her house," Papa says.

"Then they're not going to any dance," says Maman.

"Maman, we can go by ourselves," Serina says. "The church is only a few blocks away."

"I don't like it," says Papa. "I don't like this neighborhood at night, especially around this time of year when everyone suspects you're carrying Christmas present money."

I have to go to that dance. They will be so sorry if they don't let me. Santos says he'll be there. He'll be waiting for me.

Then I hear my uncle say the magic words: "I'll take them."

And Serina and I are saved.

Tonight I'm going to a grand ball with Santos. I don't have a white Cinderella dress or a fairy godmother, but I do have my sister's long red suede dress and an uncle to take me to the Christmas dance.

"Everything will be all right," Uncle Perrin says to Maman and Papa before we leave.

"You have Clara's phone number," Papa says. "Call us if you have any problems."

When we get outside, Serina lets it out: "*Mon Dye!* I'm eighteen years old and I have to have my uncle walk me to a dance six blocks away! All my friends' boyfriends are taking them to this dance! I have to ask permission to go everywhere! They don't trust me!"

"It's not that they don't trust you," Uncle Perrin tells her, wrapping a scarf around his neck. "They are raising you in a jungle. I didn't want to say this in front of your mother and father—at least not when you two want to go to this dance—but the day before yesterday I was walking and I saw this young boy from across the street pull out an Uzi and gun down this other boy. Right in front of me. The boy with the Uzi got into a car and sped away. Anybody who was in the way could have been killed. Let me tell you, I was so scared I peed on myself. When I got to your house I cried as if I knew the boy who died."

I think about my uncle crying in a house all by himself. I can picture his shoulders shaking, eyes red, slime coming out of his nose. I can see him even though I've never seen him that way before. I know this is not the first time he has seen someone get shot dead.

"Things like that always happen," Serina says, rubbing her lips together. As soon as we got outside, she put dark red lipstick on and changed her low pumps to high pointy-heeled shoes. Uncle Perrin only laughed and shook his head at her. I wanted to run back upstairs and tell my mother. I know Serina has her mind on that boy Jean-Robert, the one I saw her kissing outside the record shop. I heard her a few days ago talking on the phone to one of her girlfriends about how cute Jean-Robert is and how he's ready to buy her an engagement ring and so on.

"Shootings happen everywhere you go now," she continues. "Those things have nothing to do with me. I feel like a dog in a box with holes. I can breathe just enough to survive, but no more."

"I feel the same way," I tell her.

"Oh, Mardi!" she says. "You're only fourteen. What do you know?"

"Let Mardi have her own opinion," Uncle Perrin says to her. "And you're only a few years older than her, so how much more could you possibly know?"

Serina doesn't say anything. We stop for a traffic light. When the light changes and we begin to cross the street, she rushes ahead of us, almost tripping.

"You'll fall in those high heels!" I call after her, laughing.

A lot of kids from school and church are already there when we get to St. Joseph's. I look for Santos but don't see him.

After we check our coats, Uncle Perrin leaves Serina and me by the entrance to the gym and goes to say hello to some people. After he walks away, Serina grabs my arm and whips me around.

"Mardi, stay where I can see you. You hear me? Don't go running off without telling me like you did last year." Her sharp nails pierce through my dress. The same spot my mother grabbed me.

"All right!" I say. "*Lage-m!* Let go!"

She lets go. We're both about to say something when two of her friends run up to her.

"Seriiinaaaa!" Her friends sound like baby pigs.

"Rosslyn! Guerda!" Serina squeals back, like they haven't seen each other in years. Serina spoke to both Rosslyn and Guerda just this morning. She kisses them hello on the cheeks.

Rosslyn bends down so I can give her a kiss, too. I step back.

"Uh-oh," Rosslyn says, offended, "what's wrong with this one?"

"She's a little animal," Serina answers.

Guerda is okay but I can't stand Rosslyn. She's the one who kept calling everything I did "junk" when she was trying to teach me English. Whenever Rosslyn comes to our house, she thinks I'm her servant: "Mardi, sweetheart, could you get me a glass of water?" "I'm hot. Could you fan me, Mardi?" "Can you go buy me some gum?" Rosslyn would even ask you to wipe her butt for her if she thought you'd do it.

"Ala bèl rad!" Guerda points at my sister's dress. "What a pretty dress!"

"On sale at Kings Plaza," Serina says, proudly modeling for them.

"What about my dress?" I ask, also twirling. "It should look good because it used to belong to Serina, the queen of leftovers."

Guerda laughs. "Mardi is such a comic!"

Serina doesn't think it's funny. She reaches for me but I duck and run across the dance floor to the table where the drinks are. I take a white plastic cup, about to pour myself some diet soda, when a hand snatches the cup from me.

I jump back.

"No, I'm not Santos," Ike says. "Scared you, didn't I?"

I had forgotten all about Ike, which is a dangerous thing to do.

He licks the rim of the cup and places it gently back in my hand. Then he walks away in his oversized jeans with back pockets big enough to hold a phone book. Some of his spit gets on me, so I take a napkin and wipe him from my hand. I go to a garbage can and throw everything away, feeling for a shaky moment like Ike's spit was all over me.

I look for Jilline and find her talking to a boy on the other side of the gym. Jilline's not Catholic but she comes to the dances to meet "cuties." Her hair is in a long braided ponytail and she's wearing a spandex shirt and tight black jeans that make her look Serina's age. Her grandfather probably didn't see how she was dressed when she left the house.

Before I get a chance to walk up to Jilline, Pierre steps in front of me.

"You two look pretty," she says, smiling.

"Me and who else?"

"You and your shadow," she laughs.

I'm immediately annoyed but I manage to say thank you. Pierre's got these blue ribbons in her hair and a lime-colored lace dress that comes down to her ankles. She even has white lace gloves on.

"This is my grandmother's dress," Pierre says, as if she's explaining something very important. "She fixed it so I could wear it tonight. She got married in this dress. Three times."

"It's very nice," I say, walking around her to get to Jilline. But she follows me.

"Patrick has the flu," she says.

"That's too bad," I say.

Jilline is writing on a piece of paper when we get to her. She hands it to a boy, who smiles, puts it in his pocket, and walks away nodding like he just got a good deal on something.

"Dial those digits between three and five o'clock," Jilline calls after him. Then she notices Pierre and me.

"Hi, y'all!" she says cheerfully, and pats my arm. This is one thing I'll always like about Jilline: she's always happy to see me.

"Hi, Jilline," Pierre says. "You two look pretty."

I roll my eyes. "Let's get something to eat," I say before Pierre can tell her shadow joke again.

A few minutes later the three of us are sitting in the bleachers with plates full of potato chips and cookies.

"Oh, Jilline," I say. "We need to talk about the science report. I've almost finished writing the whole report. You said you'd do the last part and you didn't."

"Yeah, yeah," Jilline says. "Listen, I'll type up the report and make the presentation in class."

That's the easy part, I say to myself. "What about the solar house?" I ask. "I have everything we need to build it. I was thinking it could be a big house with balconies and plants—"

"Mardi, this is a science report. You really don't need the house."

"It's important to show people what we're talking about."

"True, but I don't want to talk about it now, Mardi. This is a party, ya dig? We've got time." Jilline starts dancing in her seat. "Ahhw! This my song!"

While Jilline enjoys her beat, I shove cookie after cookie in my mouth. I hadn't eaten when I left my house and didn't realize how hungry I was. My mouth is full of crumbs when I see Santos walk in. I almost choke.

"Are you okay?" Pierre asks. "Do you want me to do that hemline manure thing for you?"

"That's Heimlich maneuver," Jilline corrects her.

I shake my head, coughing out cookie bits. I take a gulp of my drink and stand up to watch Santos. First he's talking with Father Wilson. He scratches his nose twice and laughs once. Then he's with a group of boys who look older than him. He's very serious with them. He keeps nodding and stroking the corners of his mouth and chin as if he has a goatee. Then he dances with this little girl who I think is his cousin or something. Santos isn't really dancing with her as much as he's playing with her, pulling her hair and turning her around and around. The little girl looks like she's having a good time.

And so am I, just watching him.

Then she comes: The Mildred Rodriguez and her girls. I sink. Mildred Rodriguez looks beautiful, as usual, in a short black leather skirt and a tight ribbed olive turtleneck. But her friends are wearing the same clothes as the boys: plaid shirts and jeans too big for them.

Jilline sees me watching Mildred and Santos.

"You could wear something just like Mildred and look cute, too," she says.

I shake my head without looking at her. I put my plate down on the bench and go stand by the exit so Santos will see me.

Santos kisses Mildred on the cheek, then puts his arms around her shoulder. They are walking toward me.

I wait like I'm about to be shot.

But they walk right past me and out of the gym with Santos never even looking at me, as if I'm white space on the wall.

What I think?

Well, I think that's okay. It stings me, but it's okay because he's with his girlfriend–his ex-girlfriend–right? I know he remembers that he asked me to this dance, but he's with his girlfriend–ex-girlfriend–and saying hello to me could make her jealous. He's trying to let her down easy.

Yes, that makes the most sense.

I go and sit with Jilline and Pierre again. I pick my plate up and shove another cookie in my mouth.

It's an hour later and Mildred and Santos still haven't come back. I've eaten four plates of cookies and watched Serina dance with every boy in the place. Jean-Robert, who got here right after we did, cuts in on almost all of Serina's dances.

Then I see two girls I know from church, Martine and Marie-Fona. They live in the building across the street from me and both go to the same Catholic school. Martine and Marie-Fona are like twins. The way they're together in their uniforms when I see them coming out of their building every morning is the same way I always see them: whispering in each other's ears, acting shocked and surprised, with all these ridiculous expressions on their faces.

But I would like to know what they talk about. Even if it's just nonsense, they make it look exciting.

Martine and Marie-Fona are dressed better than Jilline, Pierre, and me but not as good as The Mildred Rodriguez. Martine has on a pants suit and Marie-Fona has on a skirt and blazer. They look like they're going to work at an office. They come and sit behind us on the bleachers. Jilline, Pierre, and I stop talking so we can hear what they're saying, but it's hard to hear them between their laughing and the loud music.

Then Marie-Fona taps me on the shoulder and says to me in Créole: "Are you going to Catholic school next year? Can your parents afford it?"

I know she's asking me in Créole on purpose so Jilline won't understand. The two don't get along. Last year at the dance they got into a fight and were both thrown out. Jilline kicked Marie-Fona's butt and called her a crap-faced wanna-be.

"I don't know," I answer in English.

"Well, if you're interested," Marie-Fona continues in Créole, "the high school I'm going to gives scholarships. I can get you an application."

"Yes, thank you," I say in English.

"Can you get one for me, too?" Pierre asks in Créole.

"It'll cost you . . . five dollars," Marie-Fona says. She's always taking money from Pierre.

"Why?" Pierre asks.

"Don't question me!" says Marie-Fona. "I'm doing something good for you. Do you want the information or not?"

Martine starts to laugh. Right at that moment I notice how much she looks like her mother. And Marie-Fona looks and acts like her mother, too. My mother said once she didn't care for Martine's or Marie-Fona's mother even though all three women grew up in the same neighborhood and knew each other well back in Haiti. "We used to go to school together and go to each other's houses," Maman had said. "Now they're like *abitans ki pran promosyon,* they've been promoted to the big house and don't know how to act. Because they're in New York making some money they think they're better than everyone else."

I can tell Jilline is getting irritated, waiting for them to talk English. Pierre takes a five-dollar bill out of her white plastic handbag and gives it to Marie-Fona.

"Next week after church I'll give the both of you the applications." Marie-Fona starts to say something else in Créole when Jilline interrupts.

"Excuse me," she says, "but could you please find some kind of courtesy in yourself to speak English? You know I'm not Haitian. I don't speak your language."

"So learn it," Marie-Fona finally says in English.

"I don't have to learn a damn thing!" Jilline stands up. "This is the United States. We speak English here and if you don't like it get the 'f' out."

"Oh, we weren't talking about you," Martine quickly explains. She's afraid of Jilline.

"That's not my point," Jilline says. "You both being rude and I don't appreciate it."

"So what?" says Marie-Fona.

"So what? So what?" Jilline repeats. "You know, you're lucky I have more self-control this year 'cause if I didn't I'd kick your ass like I did last year."

"I take karate lessons at my school," says Marie-Fona. "I could kill you."

"You'd need a gun to kill me," Jilline says.

"Maybe I have one," answers Marie-Fona.

"You don't have a damn thing except your alien card," Jilline says. "All you boat people leave your starving-ass countries and when you get here y'all think y'all the baked potato we've been waiting for. You treat black people who've been here hundreds of years like they've never done anything for you. It's not perfect yet, but we've at least set up this country so you could come here."

Boat people? I say to myself. Is this what Jilline thinks I am? Is this the way she sees my family and other people from the West Indies? If I had come over on a yacht or cruise ship, would I still be "boat people"? And besides, I came over on American Airlines, flew in first class on flight 658.

We're all quiet for a moment.

"Thank you," Pierre finally says to Jilline. "I thank you for all you've done."

"Oh, shut up!" Marie-Fona shouts at Pierre. To Jilline she says, "All I'm saying is I can speak a different language if I want. Like you said, this is America and it's all about what I want."

"You're just showing off," says Jilline.

"So what? Why don't you go and learn a language so you can show off, too? Créole is part of my culture."

"Can you keep your culture without being rude, Fona?" Jilline asks.

"And can you look at me without being jealous?" Marie-Fona starts to model. Pierre and Martine laugh.

"Oh, please," Jilline says, starting to smile herself. "Sit your butt down."

"Say it in Créole and I will," teases Marie-Fona.

"Well, how do you say 'Sit your butt down' in Créole?" Jilline asks.

Pierre tells her. Jilline tries to repeat it and ends up making everybody laugh, including herself, but I'm not laughing. What Jilline said wasn't at all funny to me.

I see Serina waving for me to come over to her side of the gym. I leave Jilline with the other girls and go over to my sister.

"Can you go get my coat for me?" Serina smiles at me. Jean-Robert is sitting next to her, leaning close to her like he's about to tell her something very special.

He asks Serina in French if I'm her sister.

"Yes, she's my sister," Serina answers in French, trying to be formal and proper. Oh, please! Everybody wants to be somebody tonight.

"Why do you need your coat?" I ask in English.

"I really don't need the coat," she says in Créole. "I left my lipstick in the pocket."

"Why do you need your lipstick? You going to kiss someone?"

Jean-Robert laughs. Serina bites her lower lip. That's a sign she wants to grab and shake me. But I know she won't make a move in front of him. It wouldn't be ladylike.

"Okay." I smile. "I'll go get it for you."

I can smell marijuana in the stairwell as I go to the coatroom. I never knew what it smelled like until one day Jilline pointed to a group of boys smoking it on a street corner. She told me to breathe deeply, and as we walked past them, I almost choked. It smelled awful to me, like dog *kaka,* and I couldn't understand how people could smoke that unless they were sick or something and had to.

I look up and see a group of kids giggling two floors above. One girl looks directly down at me, blowing smoke my way. I fly down a flight of stairs and run into the coatroom.

No one is in here, which is strange. There's always someone in the coatroom. As I walk to the back, I think I hear someone sniffling. I turn around but no one's there.

I find Serina's coat and take the lipstick out. I put some Ruby Red on and start kissing the air, imagining the air is Santos.

"Hey, island guuurl."

I slowly turn around.

Ike's eyes are red and he's grinning like he's lost his mind and doesn't care. "Hey, island guuurl, you looking pretty tonight," he says. But with each step he takes toward me his smile fades.

My knees shake. I back up against a rack of coats, fighting the need to pee on myself. No, I'm not going to. I won't!

He reaches me and smears the lipstick I have on with the back of his hand. I try to run past him but he grabs the collar of my dress, lifts me by the neck, and backs me past the coat racks and into the cold cement walls of the coat-room. Prepare yourself, Mardi. I close my eyes.

"Open them!" he yells.

I look into his eyes. They are brown and round and wet, and if he wasn't holding me like this now, they could have even been pretty.

"M-my b-big brother, Aaron, he's dead in prison now," Ike says. "Today he's been dead a month. H-he was suppose to come home and help me but the punks stab him with scissors like a vampire 'cause he got tired of b-being a girl for the men. He's dead, Mardi! What I'm gonna do about Daddy? A-Aaron was suppose to come home and help . . . me. . . ." Ike starts to cry. And I start crying, too.

I'm scared.

I feel sorry for him.

But I'm scared.

I remember Haiti.

I remember the cornfields.

I remember there was no one around and how thirsty I was.

I remember what happened there.

I remember not saying anything.

I begin to growl.

"What do you want?" I yell at him.

"It's my birthday, today, Mardi," he says, loosening his

grip on me. "Sing me 'Happy Birthday.' That's all I want from you."

"Leave me alone!"

"I'm not gonna hurt you," Ike says, letting go of me. "Sing me 'Happy Birthday.' "

"No!" I yell. "No!" My knees are shaking so much I fall to the floor. Ike steps back, looking at me like he doesn't understand what's gotten into me.

I can't run past him but I can still protect myself. I curl up into a ball and cross my legs as tightly as I can, fighting with my arm every which way. My hand grabs hold of a wooden stick leaning against the wall. I swing it at Ike. When I keep missing him, I start hitting myself in the face and yell, "Stop! Leave me alone! Enough! Stop!" I realize what I'm doing but can't stop.

"You freaking out!" Ike says. He grabs the stick away, throwing it across the room. "Shut up, Mardi! Stop freaking out on me!"

"What go on here?" It's Uncle Perrin.

"Man, I ain't do nothing," Ike says.

My uncle rushes over to me and touches the lipstick and bruises on my face. "What you do to my baby?" he yells at Ike.

"I said I ain't do nothing." Ike backs away.

"Oh, yeah, miss-ter?" He grabs Ike by the collar and shoves him against the wall.

"Get off me!" Ike yells. "I ain't do nothing!"

"Leave him alone," I say, but no one hears me. "Leave him alone!" I say louder.

"You hit?" Uncle says to Ike. "You hit? Where you hand? I gonna cut off hand you hit Mardi!"

"He didn't hit me!" I say.

"Who hit?"

"Me! I did this! I did this to myself!"

Uncle Perrin slowly lets Ike go, not sure who to believe. He pushes Ike toward the door. "You not better come back here, miss-ter."

"You crazy!" Ike tells him. "You must be crazy to be talking to me like that. Don't nobody talk to me like that and live. I ain't even hit the b–"

"Yeah, I crazy," Uncle Perrin says. "I crazy to beating you up! *Frekan!* Fresh boy!"

Ike grabs his crotch. "Suck me!" He runs out the door.

Uncle Perrin helps me to my feet. "Did he do anything to you?"

I shake my head.

"Are you sure?"

I'm not sure of anything. "Please don't tell my mother."

He doesn't make me any promises. He leads me out of the hot coatroom, out of the building, to a cooler place outside.

Something begins to melt in me the days following the dance. A chunk of ice solid as steel. I feel like I'm finally beginning to understand the answer to a hard question, like I felt when English became a language I understood. It's good to know when someone's on your side. Maybe they can't really save you from anything, but it's still good knowing they would if they could. It's also good not to hate people, especially people who keep proving they love you.

I blamed Uncle Perrin for everything and he's the one who's always defended me since he got here. What would Ike have done to me if my uncle hadn't been there? What would I have done to myself?

I am so ashamed.

I needed to hate someone and he was the next best thing to Aunt Widza. But it's no fun hating Aunt Widza.

She always thought I was joking, but Uncle Perrin, he took me seriously, he always did.

The night we get home from the St. Joseph's dance, I go into the bathroom with a piece of paper, scissors, and markers. I cut out a heart, then fold it in half so it looks like an upside-down tear. On one side of the heart I draw a circle with an unhappy face and write my name above it. On the other side I draw a circle with a happy face and write above it: *Mardi after Monnonk comes to New York. I am sorry.*

As I tiptoe to the living room, where Uncle Perrin is asleep, I pass a picture of Jesus Christ—one of many we have in the house. But this picture is electric and lights up. Someone gave it to my mother a few days ago instead of cash for a party she cooked for. The eyes glow in the dark and follow me. They feel like fingers pressing on my back, so I hurry to where my uncle is sleeping before the lips of the picture begin to move, too.

I slip the card under his pillow, and the next morning I find the same card under my pillow. I start to think that maybe he didn't want it, that maybe a card is not enough to make up for how I treated him. But when I open it my name is crossed out above both circles and replaced with his name. The smiling circle says: *Perrin after Mardi finds her senses. I am happy.*

I kiss the card and slip it inside my pillowcase.

I wake up this morning and say good morning to Uncle Perrin. He places his hand on my head and smiles back at me. Aunt Widza comes in and without a word rests her head on Uncle Perrin's shoulder. She looks so tired, like a baby waking up from sleep. She takes us both by the waist and brings us together. I smell stale sweet cologne on Monnonk's pajamas and I feel the soft polyester fur on Matant's robe. I'm dizzy, a good dizzy. I could jump out of an airplane right now and believe the earth is a bed of feathers.

"What's going on here?" my mother asks. She and my father are standing in the hallway.

"Nothing," I say.

"Everything," Aunt Widza says.

Later I'm sitting at the kitchen table eating cornmeal with carrots that Uncle Perrin cooked. My father is having coffee and talking to him.

"It is hopeless," Papa says, waving his hand like he's trying to get rid of an annoying fly. "The situation in Haiti is hopeless. They take one step forward and then three steps back. I don't see when or how me and Polette can go back to Jacmel and build that house—that is, if our land is still there. Every week I hear stories of the same plot of land being sold over and over to different people. What a racket!"

"Papa," I say, "what would the house look like?"

"Ah, Mardi," my father says, leaning back and smiling at the ceiling like there is a good memory there. "It's beautiful. Like your grandmother's house in Port-au-Prince but a little different. Two floors, balconies. The roof would be a little round, lots of room . . . Yes, and you know our land is not far from the ocean. . . . But I don't know, I would have been prepared to go there this year to lay the foundation at least, but . . ." He waves his hand again at the invisible fly.

"Don't be such a pessimist," Uncle Perrin tells him, scooping a spoonful of cornmeal into his mouth.

"Well, what am I supposed to be right now?" says my father. "Happy? I could put you in hell and you'd still come out with some sunshine in your pocket and tell me it's not so bad down there."

"Everything has its moment."

"It seems we've been in a bad moment for a very long time. I want a good one to start already."

I watch my uncle carefully. Every move he makes is now graceful to me. I want to clap and say bravo when he sits, when he leans his head back to think and wrinkles the left side of his face, and when he pats his chest as he's making a point.

He even smells good.

"Haiti," my father continues, "will finish for certain with this coup and embargo. What a country it was, so sweet long ago. I can never show my children what my childhood was like. There was this joke we used to say when I was growing up. It goes, Long ago, instead of throwing rocks at each other, when people were fighting, they would throw meat because there was so much to eat." Papa laughs.

"It's your country," Aunt Widza says. She's sitting by the kitchen window making herself mayonnaise cracker sandwiches. "You'll always love it. You'll always see the good in what is yours."

Serina walks in with her forehead wrapped in a white cloth. She smells like Vicks and castor oil. "My Saridon pills are all gone. I have such a headache."

"How could you have a headache?" asks my father. "I know they didn't serve alcohol last night at the dance."

Uncle Perrin and I keep silent. We don't say how Serina left the dance early with Jean-Robert and how we had to wait almost an hour for her to return because we didn't want to go home without her. When she finally showed up, she said she had a run in her pantyhose and had gone to the store to buy new ones.

Please. Like we're stupid.

"There are other things besides alcohol that can give you a headache, Papa," she says, sitting at the table with a cup of hot water and a box of chamomile tea. "The music was so loud. I was right by the speakers."

My mother comes in.

"Mardi, get out of the kitchen and go to the room."

"Grandmère is still sleeping."

"Then go into the bathroom and shut the door. There's a bucket of clothes in the bathtub that need to be rinsed out now."

I look at Uncle Perrin.

"Go on," he says. "Your mother is talking to you."

I leave my breakfast at the table and go to the bathroom. I turn the bathtub water on high so Maman will think I can't hear. When I shut the water off, there's shouting and crying.

"But it's not mine!" I hear Serina say.

"Who do you think you're raising your voice at?" my father says.

"I found this under your bed!" my mother says.

"What were you doing under my bed?" Serina asks.

"What do you mean what was she doing under your bed?" says my father. "Isn't she your mother? Isn't this her house?"

"I have no privacy!"

"Why do you need privacy?" asks my mother. "Are you hiding something?"

"Don't you know when we first came into this country," says my father, "your mother and I shared an apartment with five other people and a bathroom with two floors?"

"I don't know where that condom came from!"

Condom? Maman found a condom under Serina's bed? They're going to kill her!

"It was in the sandals you borrowed from me," my mother says. "If you were as smart as you think you are, you would have gotten the sandals yourself when I asked you for them."

"But, Maman, I'm telling you I don't know where—"

"Listen, Serina," says my mother, "you're eighteen years old, and by law in this country that makes you an adult. Whatever *malpròpte* you do on your own, keep it outside this house. Don't bring your dirty dealings in here to corrupt the other members of this family."

The other member being me.

"It's mine," Uncle Perrin says.

"What?" says Maman.

"I'm sorry, it's mine."

Silence.

"Listen," Papa says. "You're a grown man, Perrin. I can't tell you what to do, but please keep your things in a better place. I'm raising daughters in this house, not boys."

"Yes, I'm sorry."

I shut the door when my mother marches past the bathroom. They leave Serina alone and don't say much else to Uncle Perrin. Even if Serina had admitted the condom was hers, shouldn't they be happy that she's at least protecting herself?

The next day I go to the library and read a book on sexually transmitted diseases. I don't have any symptoms of anything. Maybe I should get tested at the family clinic. But they'd need permission from an adult. Uncle Perrin maybe? That might work. But that'll mean I'll have to tell him.

I don't want to think about it, so I won't.

Next subject: Christmas.

As I walk home from the library, I force myself to think about the holidays and how this might be a nice one. My mother likes to open Christmas presents late on Christmas Eve, before she and my father go to midnight mass at St. Joseph's.

The presents stacked up under our tree are the only things keeping it from falling. Papa got it from the reusable-things yard and won't throw it away because "if it weren't for the stand's two missing legs, and a few missing branches, the tree is practically new." Maman warns him that this will be our last holiday with it; either she buys a new one next year or there won't be a tree at all.

On Christmas Eve we're all in the living room opening

our presents. Maman does the most Christmas shopping. Her gifts never go to waste and they're almost always expensive. She's probably run up the limit on her credit cards, but then again, my mother could find a sale on the moon. Paying full price and committing murder carry almost the same weight with her. This year is no different, even though she's not working at the factory. She gives Grandmère an electric foot massager; there's a complete set of tools from Sears for my father; Uncle Perrin gets a fancy winter coat from Macy's; Aunt Widza, boots; Serina, steam hair curlers; and me, Maman gives me a CD radio with a double tape deck.

"If you break that," she says to me, smiling, "I'll break your head."

I thank her, wondering how she knew this is what I wanted. Then I remember the sex tape thing, when I was cleaning the house and Serina suspected that I had done something wrong. I had told Serina I was cleaning the house because I wanted a CD player for Christmas. She must have told Maman. Sometimes a sister's big mouth can be useful.

Grandmère Adda and Serina each give me a blouse, and I get pajamas from Aunt Widza.

My father gives me three dollars: a two-dollar bill and two fifty-cent pieces. "Don't spend them, Mardi," he says. "They're for good luck."

Since I don't have any money, I made pop-up Christmas cards for everyone except Uncle Perrin. I give Uncle Perrin a rock I painted red and blue, the colors of the Haitian flag.

"A rock?" says Serina. "What kind of a present is that to give to someone?"

"I got this rock," I tell her, "from the front gates of Grandmère's house."

"I like it very much," Uncle Perrin says. "This is as big and heavy as Mardi's heart."

"You mean as her head," Maman says. And everyone laughs, this time even me. Last year it was only Maman, Papa, Serina, and me, and Christmas Eve felt like any other day.

Uncle Perrin hands out his gifts to everyone: slippers with cartoon heads at the toes.

"Oh, Perrin, how very nice of you," my mother tells him, looking at her Miss Piggy slippers. She'll never wear them.

"Yes," Aunt Widza says, kissing hers, Wonder Woman. "My brother wants me to have warm feet."

Serina has Betty Boop; she slips them on right away. Grandmère gets Wilma Flintstone, and my father, Fred Flintstone.

But I get something else besides my Batgirl slippers. Uncle Perrin hands me another box.

"Two presents?" I ask.

He nods.

It's a deluxe collector's edition of Scrabble.

"I know you like to play with pictures," he says, "and I thought you might also enjoy doing that with words."

"I like it." It's something new to do on boring winter weekends.

"How do you know how to play Scrabble?" I ask Uncle

Perrin. I learned how to play because Jilline has the game and we used to play dirty-word Scrabble, which Jilline always won.

"I learned to play in the camps in Cuba," he says. "I got friendly with that soldier who gave me the guitar. He spoke a little French and I could speak a little Spanish. Sometimes he'd arrange for me to get out of the camps by cleaning the bathrooms. I got extra food for Pélé and his mother when I did that." Uncle Perrin rarely talks about the camps in Guantánamo.

"Aaahhh! In any case, you shouldn't have spent the little money you have!" Grandmère says.

"Yes, and you're not even working," says Maman.

"Well, he'll be working soon," Papa says.

"How? Perrin's found a job?" asks Grandmère.

"I finally found him a job," my father says proudly. "Maman, remember Franco Lepanelle? He lived across the street from Matant Oriel's house? We went to school together? The one a car hit and he always walked with a limp after that?"

"Oh, yes," Grandmère says. "That happened in front of our house. I thought the car had hit you at first and came running outside. I told you boys not to play soccer in the street. Yes, I remember Franco. Madan Rose's boy. He was such a nice, timid boy. His nose was always making sauce."

"Yes, that's him, and his nose is still runny. Well, I don't know if I ever told you, but he's head of building maintenance where I work. Last week he was telling me one of his people quit and he needed a replacement. I told him about Perrin and he was too happy. He remembers Perrin when Perrin was a boy. Perrin will start work as soon as all his papers are in order."

Everyone congratulates Uncle Perrin except me. He's going to work, he'll have money, and then he'll find his own place and move out–just like I wanted.

What I think?

I think sometimes the scary part isn't the waiting and the hoping, it's the getting what I ask for. Like with Pélé. He has three presents under the Christmas tree. When I go to gather them, Uncle Perrin tells me, "Leave them. I'm going to visit Pélé tomorrow. Do you want to come?"

The next morning Uncle Perrin and I take the E train to the last stop. Uncle Perrin has never come here by train, and we're lost until we ask directions from a man with a long beard who's selling oils and incense. He tells us the dollar vans would be the fastest way. The van we get is packed with four rows of people and their bags of presents. The windows don't open, the heat is on high, gospel music is blaring, but the driver curses at every car that dares cut him off.

I suppose the ride could have taken us no more than ten minutes except the van has to go through this thick net of stores and serious shoppers who can't even rest on Christmas day. Half an hour later, we're dropped off at the corner of a quiet street in Queens Village. Uncle Perrin looks at the address in his hand and points in front of him.

While the other houses on the block have maybe one or two lights, Pélé's house has blinking decorations and icicle lights on the rooflines, archways, windows, the front porch, and the bushes. I feel like I'm looking at a dollhouse, the kind I see in store windows that makes me stop and wish I could shrink and go in and live in it.

Uncle Perrin rings the doorbell. A few moments later an old lady with a cane opens the door. She's the older woman in the picture taped on our front door. When she sees Uncle Perrin, she drops her cane and covers her mouth with both hands.

"Oh, Perrin!" she says. "Thank God for you. I knew you'd come. Come in! Come in!"

"Matant Carmel," Uncle Perrin says, kissing and hugging her. "You know I wouldn't leave you like that."

"Yes, that's true, that's true. I couldn't find your number and I've been looking and looking for it. In all this looking I found a passport from 1968, but no number. I even found a ring I lost three years ago, but not your phone number! Let me take your coats. And is this your Mardi?"

"Yes, it is," Uncle Perrin says.

"The one Pélé keeps talking about?"

Pélé talks about me?

"That boy," Matant Carmel says, leading us to her living room. "If he's not talking about his papa Perrin he's talking about his cousin Mardi. He talks about you more than he does his own mother."

"It's very hard for him," Uncle Perrin says.

"Yes, yes, I don't force him. I let him be. Let me call him. Pélé, honey? Come see who's here for you!" She limps out of the room.

I sink into the soft leather sofa. The house smells like clothes fresh from the dryer. I wish I could take off my boots. The carpet must feel like a stuffed teddy bear's tummy.

"It's a pretty house."

Uncle Perrin nods. "Her children are all grown. One is a doctor."

The walls have rows and rows of diplomas and pictures of Matant Carmel and her family. It starts off on one end with what looks like a picture of a young Matant Carmel and then a picture of a young man. Then there's a wedding picture of Matant Carmel and this young man, and with every picture a child is added until the family has five children. There are baby, communion, graduation, and wedding pictures throughout. Then there's a line of family pictures minus one child, and after that point the one child is gone. Later on when the kids are grown, another child is gone and there are three. Then the father disappears, leaving Matant Carmel alone in a picture that seems like it was taken not too long ago.

Pélé comes running into Uncle Perrin's arms. "Papa Perrin!" He's still in his pajamas. "I have a present for you!" His teeth are growing back.

"We have presents for you, too," Uncle Perrin tells him.

"But I have a present for everyone! Come to my room to see! You come, too, Mardi!" He takes both our hands and leads us upstairs to his room. I've seen this room before. The kids on Saturday-morning TV have it, too: carpet, dresser, desk, curtains that match the bedsheets. The room is huge—too big for a little boy. Pélé jumps up and down on his bed.

"See my bed? I can jump on it! It's really soft! Come jump with me, Papa Perrin! Come jump with me, Mardi!"

If Uncle Perrin wasn't here, I would have jumped with him to see whose hand would touch the ceiling first. Pélé can't stop talking. He shows me his toys and says I can take one home if I like since I don't have many toys at my house. He shows me his closet full of clothes and offers to give me some for any boy dolls I have. Then he gives us our presents: cards he made himself, misspelling our names.

Before we leave, Matant Carmel gives Uncle Perrin a gallon of *kremas,* a thick, sweet, milky coconut drink with rum in it, like eggnog. *Kremas* is not very hard to make but very easy to mess up. She must really like Uncle Perrin because nobody gives just anybody a gallon of the stuff.

On our train ride back to Brooklyn I sit close to Uncle Perrin. "Uncle, Pélé will never forget his mother or the camp or Haiti."

"I know," he says. "None of us will."

I lean back and look out the window at the darkness speeding by. I feel my pocket and take out the orange building block Pélé gave me the morning he left my house. I was going to give it back to him but I'm glad I forgot. I'll put it in the same velvet bag as my grandmother's rocks.

The week between Christmas and New Year's, I start work on the solar house for the science report. Jilline and her grandfather went to South Carolina, so again she's not going to be much help.

I take a flat piece of wood the size of a pizza box, which I found in my father's reusable-things yard. I paint it brown, the same kind of brown on a leaf when it's changing color in the fall. I cut and slice pieces of white foam board to make the foundation and the first floor of my house. There's going to be a large living room by the entrance, a place to eat, and another open space I haven't decided what to do with yet. Maybe it will be a library. Libraries need lots of light.

When I'm done, I place everything on a small table by the window in the living room. Over the next few days I divide the floor space and put up the walls. By New Year's Eve there's a backyard and a *cha cha* tree.

166

On New Year's Eve my family stays up until midnight to say prayers. Grandmère Adda makes *likè* for us to drink with bread and cake. Maman has us all wear something yellow for good luck.

The ball in Times Square drops, and on TV Dick Clark announces that a new year is beginning.

"Bòn ane! Bòn sante!" we all say. A good year and good health to everyone! We hug and kiss each other hello because this is the first time we're seeing each other this year.

Grandmère heats a pot of fresh pineapples in water and, with Aunt Widza's help, pours bits and pieces of pineapple everywhere. She makes everyone wash their face with a chunk of pineapple. I wash my face twice. Aunt Widza eats her pineapple chunks.

On New Year's Day we have the traditional big pot of pumpkin soup to celebrate Haiti's 1804 independence from France.

"The first black republic in the world," my father reminds us every year.

"And the first successful slave revolution in the New World," Uncle Perrin adds.

Lots of people from church and people who live in our building come to our house for a bowl because my grandmother makes the best soup *joumou*. Grandmère, Papa, and Maman are so busy talking and handing out bowls that they don't notice Serina slipping out of the house.

I borrow my father's small folding table and set it up in the bedroom. I put my Scrabble game on top of it, then go to the living room and invite Uncle Perrin and Aunt Widza for a game.

Two games later, Uncle Perrin is winning. He's spelling words like "victory" and "success" in English. Aunt Widza spells the word "no" three times and then *"gâter,"* which means "to spoil" in French. I spell the word "saints" in Spanish.

"Santos," says Aunt Widza. "You do like the boy."

"Who's Santos?" Uncle Perrin asks.

"He is Mr. Amorez's son," says Aunt Widza. "A nice-looking boy, but–"

"No," I say. "I only spelled the word because the letters were there."

"Mardi," she says, "we only spell out the names of those we love or hate."

"Maybe I hate him," I say.

"I thought I was the one you hated," she says.

"No, you're mistaken, Widza," says my uncle. "She hates me."

"You know I don't hate you two," I say, trying to hide a smile.

"But seriously, Mardi," Aunt Widza says, "that boy Santos is what, fourteen? Fifteen? The other day he comes into his father's store, he makes sure no one is looking, blows me a kiss, then licks his lips at me."

"Maybe his lips were dry," I say.

"Then he should carry Vaseline on him. I'm old enough to be his mother. It's the way he did it. . . . When I didn't respond he crumpled a piece of paper and threw it at me."

"The boy must like you, Widza," says Uncle Perrin. "If

he keeps bothering you or makes you uncomfortable, tell his father."

"It's not me I'm worried about," she says. She looks right into me and I wonder if she can see my spot of jealousy over Santos paying her some attention. But he was only playing with her. Nothing will come of it.

Feeling reassured, I look at the letter I've been holding in my hand. It's a V, and I have an I and an O. Then I see, right there in the game, the other letters I've been looking for: "late."

My hands tremble. It feels like someone is opening my chest and letting cold air in. But I can trust my uncle and my aunt. They've always listened, right . . . ?

What I think?

Yes, what do *you* think?

I place "vio" in front of "late."

Violate.

I straighten my back, place my feet together, join my knees, and put my hands on my thighs, palms facing down.

"Why did you spell that, Mardi?" asks my uncle.

My eyes are wet. "Because no other words will fit!" I yell. Then, "I'm sorry." I start to move the letters around, but Uncle Perrin takes my hand away and looks for something hidden in me.

"What happened to you?" he asks.

I am twelve years old.
Serina and I are in the truck with some other people on our

way to the airport. Some men with hoods and guns came knocking on our door the week before, looking for Uncle Perrin, who wasn't there. That's when Grandmère said it was time for us to leave the country.

The truck moves up and down hills and mountainsides. At one point, I can see all of Port-au-Prince. The morning sun shining on the city makes it look like there are diamonds down there somewhere. But I still want to get on the plane that'll take me to my mother and father in New York, not because I'm scared, but because I want to be high in the sky and want to see the buildings in New York that I hear are bigger than Mount Laseil near Kenscoff.

It is a Sunday morning and we are all dressed like we're going to church. On the road we pass barefoot women carrying large buckets of water on their heads, darting here and there, trying to stay off the road. There are sick, skinny dogs with black dots on their bodies, looking like someone scraped the fur off them. . . . I smell fire. Someone is burning garbage under the wooden bridge we are passing. I see a pig greedily eating up whatever it is that pigs eat up in the garbage.

I close my eyes and lean on my sister's shoulder. She tells me not to fall asleep and I shake my head. I will never sleep.

The truck stops and I open my eyes again.

Mon Dye, *the old woman across from me says. My God. I hear her heartbeat and everybody else's. I look toward the front and I can see the driver and several men talking. One of the men puts this big long gun against the driver's head.*

Do you know such and such? *they ask, but the driver keeps shaking his head. Then I hear Uncle Perrin's name.*

Our driver says, I am taking everyone to church.

170

What church? they want to know.

I have the paper here, our driver says.

Move slowly, they warn him.

But instead of reaching for a paper, our driver steps on the gas. Everyone gets on the floor of the truck. My sister is on top of me. I hear gunshots. We are shaken like marbles in a box.

Imbecile *driver! someone shouts out. You're going to get us all killed!*

La vie! La vie, mon Dye! *another yells.*

The truck crashes into something. When I get out, I see we've hit a tree. One boy is shot in the leg; another man is bleeding, not moving, on the ground. My sister grabs my hand and we run into the thick stalks of corn. My heart does mini-explosions one after the other.

We run across the cornfields and into the woods. I feel blood coming out of my nose and wipe it away with the back of my hand. Someone waves to us ahead; it's our driver.

Come, he tells us, you can hide here.

We all go inside a small house made of leaves, hidden behind a thick row of trees. There are other people from the truck and more I don't recognize.

We need to stay here for a while, our driver says.

What about our flight? a woman asks. My plane leaves at noon! I was supposed to meet my husband in New York! She starts crying.

There, there, cheri, *an old woman comforts her. It's better to be late and alive than early and dead.*

Someone's transistor radio says that the airport is closed for security reasons. We have corn and salty raw codfish for breakfast, lunch, and dinner. And the next day is just the same, only we're running out of drinking water. Everyone sits on the ground in a circle, not talking and, I suspect, taking very small breaths of air. Small birds tease us by flying in and out of the hut. Look at us, they seem to say, we are free.

Until one bird gets too close and ends up being someone's supper.

The day after that I wake up early, still thirsty from last night's codfish dinner. Everyone is still asleep. I stand up and feel the cool early-morning breeze on my arms and legs. I yawn.

I'm so thirsty.

Quietly I step outside the hut with my sister's thermos. It's so quiet that I'm not afraid. I stand on top of a small hill, trying to remember where I saw a little stream when we were running across the fields. I'll surprise everyone with water when they wake up.

I didn't think it would take me long, but I forget where I'm going. In a while I'm going around in circles, it feels. I think about yelling out for help but can't tell how far I am from my sister—even if I jump up. The corn is taller than me in lots of places.

Then I get lucky. I find a path in the field and spot the stream. But when I get there, it isn't the stream I saw earlier. I find a muddy dug-up open tunnel with puddles of water.

I'll just go back before anyone wakes up.

"Ey, ti cheri," a voice calls out. "Hey, little honey, are you lost?" A man with a rifle is leaning against a tree to my far left. He winks at me.

"N-no," I answer. "M-my sister sent me for some water."

"Is your sister pretty?" the cornfield man asks.

"I—I don't know," I say, backing away into the field.

Before he can say anything else, I'm running and tripping and running again, pushing the corn aside so I can get through. But the cornfield man catches me.

"Leave me alone!" I beg. "Let me go. . . . no!" He drags me by the arm to a ravine where there's a bald man and two boys not much older than Serina. One boy has on red sneakers and the other black combat boots. I recognize the bald man. He's the one who put his rifle to the driver's head.

There's two women in the ravine. They sit on the ground with their hands tied behind their backs to a pole.

"Here's a little toy I found." The cornfield man throws me in. I land on my face.

"You're always collecting things," Bald Head says, counting a pile of money on the ground in front of him.

"She's just a child," the older woman shouts. "You have to let her go!"

Red Sneakers points a gun at the woman's throat. She's old enough to be his mother, but he says the nastiest things to her. He's even touching her chest as he talks.

"Please don't hurt my mother," the younger woman tells him.

"Shut up, Carlen!" her mother says.

"Yes, shut up, Carlen." Combat Boots laughs softly. He plays with Carlen's long wavy black hair. Carlen and her mother are dirty. Their clothes are ripped and they look very tired. I don't know what they are doing here, tied up in this big hole with these two men and boys. I have heard the president was almost killed and that's when the trouble began. But what does that have to do with me? I just want to get back to my sister.

Then the cornfield man tells me to lie down. I lie down,

holding on tight to my sister's thermos. I'll get in trouble if I lose it. He lies down next to me and puts his hands on my throat and chest as if he's a doctor examining me for a pain I have.

"You're skinny." Cornfield Man smiles at me. His breath stinks. His yellow teeth crisscross from the gums. He lifts my dress and sticks his rifle in my panties. It feels like ice against me.

"Oh, God! Leave her alone, you devils!" Carlen's mother cries.

Red Sneakers knocks her across the forehead with his gun.

"Mamaaaa!" Carlen yells. Combat Boots blindfolds her and covers her mouth with his hands.

"If you can't keep them quiet I'll kill them myself," Bald Head says. Now, with the money counted, he's lying in the shade with a hat half-covering his face. He hums along with a Spanish song that's playing on the small radio beside him.

Cornfield Man kisses me on my forehead. It's cold on the inside where he pushes his rifle in. My stomach is doing a roller-coaster dance.

What I think?

I think I'm going to throw up and ruin my pretty Easter dress.

Then he pulls the trigger. I jump. He laughs. I'm not dead. I wish I were. He pulls the trigger again and again, laughing harder each time. He unbuckles his pants and hugs me. Now the rifle is gone and I feel something different. It hurts just as much, but Cornfield Man enjoys himself.

Can't he see my face? If he could, he would stop, because he's a grown man and I am twelve years old and he should know better than to be doing this to me. Can't he see my face? Why won't he look at my eyes or wipe the blood coming from my nose?

When he is finished, he pulls his pants up and stretches. Just as he yawns, a bullet comes through his chest. Cornfield Man falls on me again. This time good and dead, I hope. Whoever is trying to save my life now is too late.

Girls are nothing. Look what a man can do to them.

I can't see anything with Cornfield Man on top of me. I hear shots again and a woman screaming. I scream, too, but I don't think anyone hears me.

I wait a long while until the shooting stops. I push him off me and stand up. My dress is ruined anyway with Cornfield Man's blood. The bald-headed man is gone. Red Sneakers and Combat Boots lie on the ground. Carlen is crying, still blindfolded. Her mother is slumped on the pole, eyes closed.

I take a machete that's lying on the ground and cut the cloth tied around Carlen's wrists. She doesn't get up to run. She doesn't take her blindfold off. I do. Carlen bends over, puts her head in her hands, and cries.

"Your mother's dead," I say.

Carlen cries harder, nodding, her long and wavy black hair in knots all over her face.

"T-today is the f-first year since m-my father died. W-we were only going t-to visit his grave. . . ."

How sad.

"I have to go," I say. "Do you want to come with me?"

"What's your name?" She finally looks up at me, trying to find my name in my face. Carlen is a very pretty woman, even with her heart aching like that, even with her eyes red and snot coming out of her nose.

"Mardi," I say.

"Mardi?" Carlen repeats. "Today is a Tuesday. You poor child, what a thing to witness on the day of your name."

Carlen calls me a poor child. She's the one who's an orphan now. "Do you want to come with me or not?" I say, irritated.

"I don't want to get you into more trouble, Mardi. Go. I'll find my way out."

"What about your mother?"

"Go, Mardi. I will be all right, and so will you. I will pray for you."

"Au revoir," I say. I take my sister's thermos and climb out of the ravine. When I turn around, Carlen is gone.

"Go!" I hear her voice say from somewhere. "Go, Mardi, and be careful! Merci! *"*

On my way I find the stream. I wash the blood off my dress and fill the thermos with water. The funny thing is, I don't get lost going back.

I tell them.

I tell them what happened to me. So now they know. The room is quiet except for the voices in the kitchen enjoying my grandmother's New Year's soup. Aunt Widza has tears running down her cheeks. Uncle Perrin wipes his away.

"I knew that . . . there was something wrong, from the moment I saw you at the airport. I knew something had changed."

"Mardi, you've put your heart in our bare hands and I will hold it as if I'm holding the last drops of water on Earth," says Aunt Widza. "Nothing is bad in you, no one— no experience can turn you into something without your permission. Look at me. I am also like you. This bad thing happened to me, too."

I stare at her, not wanting to believe.

"Widza, don't," says Uncle Perrin. "She doesn't need to hear this—"

"This is exactly what she needs to hear!" Aunt Widza snaps back. "You all try to keep it quiet. You all try to cover this fire that's in my mouth!"

"Widza, please," Uncle begs her. "Not now."

"Dear, dear, brother," she says. "How can it be more painful for you than it was for me? Mardi, for you it was a stranger in the cornfields. For me it was my godfather, one of my father's cousins. He was my tutor. I took lessons from him in grammar, history, science. . . . He taught me other things as well. In that one year I learned more than a woman twice my age. But one day I had had enough of his—his teaching, his hands! And I almost killed him with a machete. He told everyone that I was trying to hurt him because he wouldn't let me kiss him. And do you know who everyone believed, including your grand-mother and your father? Him! They believed him over me because my mother had caught me once kissing a boy on the cheek. A sixteen-year-old girl like me had no power over such a respectable man as my godfather, an educator and a former diplomat. Your uncle Perrin was the only one who believed me. So I believe all the things you say and I hate the person who would cause you such pain."

"I'll have to tell Maman and Papa?" I ask after a while.

"When you're ready," Uncle Perrin says.

"I can't. I'll be different to them."

"Do you want us to tell them?" Aunt Widza asks.

"Yes," I answer. "Yes."

She places one arm around my shoulder and gently pushes my head toward her. She puts her other hand in mine. She squeezes and I, finally, squeeze back.

The next day I sit by myself in the room, waiting, holding a tidal wave inside me.

Tick.

Tick.

Tick.

Uncle Perrin and Aunt Widza are talking about me in the living room. Everyone listens. For the first few minutes I don't hear anything. Then:

Grandmère: "Aaaaaahhhhhhhhhh!"

Maman: *"Kisa?* What do you mean?"

Papa: "I don't understand you!"

Serina: "How? When . . . how?"

Grandmère: "Aaaaaahhhhhhhhhh!"

I get up, unlock the bedroom door, and slowly walk to the living room. Their eyes go from me to their hands and for a very long moment they say nothing. For once.

Serina jumps up and runs to me. "Oh, Mardi," she moans, trying to gather me up in her arms. "I am so sorry. If I had known, if we had known . . ."

Grandmère looks at me like I am already lying dead in a coffin.

"Don't look at Mardi that way," Aunt Widza tells her. "Don't you all look at her the same way you look at me."

My father is shaking. His hands begin to tremble so much that he rubs his face, and when that doesn't help he shoves them in his pocket. He looks at my mother, who has not said a word. For the first time in my life my mother is speechless. The two of them suddenly look tired and twice their age. They face me.

"Se pa te fòt mwen," I say from inside Serina's arms. "It wasn't my fault."

I stand very still. I look at a faded painting of Jesus Christ on our wall. This one has dark skin, dreadlocks, and green eyes. My father found it at the reusable-things yard. The Jesus's green eyes move, look at me, then at the top of everyone's heads, then settle back in place, looking out the window. There is a small smile on the painting's lips.

Papa takes a deep breath. "You have a lot of courage, Mardi, so young, and all this time you suffered alone." He's standing next to me and puts his hand on my head. The warmth of it reaches to my feet.

I start crying.

"You don't have to cry," Serina says. "You're safe now. You're home."

"But home is not always the first place you find peace," says my mother. "Let her be."

Serina takes me into the bedroom and sits me down. She wipes my eyes with the ends of her skirt.

"Blow," she says, but I shake my head because I don't want to leave any slime on her clothes. She sits across from me, staring.

"Don't look at me like that," I tell her. "I don't want you or anybody to look at me like I'm dying."

"Mardi . . ." She starts crying again and so do I. I feel myself slipping to the floor. Serina catches me and puts me safely back on the bed.

The following Friday I don't go to school–the first time I've ever been absent. Instead, my mother takes me to the clinic to get tested for AIDS and other sexually transmitted diseases.

On our bus ride there my mother is very quiet, staring straight ahead, gently circling each bead of a broken rosary between her fingers. When she finally looks at me, she presses her lips together, fighting to keep something in. I can see now she has the same piece of ice in her that I have in me. Uncle Perrin and Aunt Widza are slowly melting mine; this is crushing hers. I reach inside my pocket and hand her my father's red handkerchief. She wipes her eyes, then gives me back the handkerchief, holding on to my hand a few moments longer than she needs to.

The doctor at the clinic is a nice woman who lets me call her by her first name, Marisol. She's young and I like her right away. She has the same long wavy black hair as Carlen, the woman from the cornfields.

"This isn't going to hurt," Marisol promises when she's telling me about the tests she'll be doing. Later I see Marisol, my mother, and another doctor talking in the hallway. Marisol comes over to me while Maman continues to talk with the other doctor, who's patting my mother's shoulder.

"We'll soon know the results of the tests we took," Marisol says. "But right now I prescribe: go home, get under the covers, put in your favorite video, and eat ice cream till it makes you so happy you scream."

I smile, but she can see I'm not in the mood.

"Look, sweetie." Marisol sits next to me. She places her warm hands on top of my fists. "We're not going to know all the results right away. But if you need to talk about anything that's happened or happening, we have counselors here. And you can talk to me because I'm a counselor, too. You don't have to hurt yourself anymore." She circles a black mark on my hand. "No more of this. It will stop now. We're all going to take care of you."

Marisol hands me her card, then pats my knee and walks back to my mother and the other doctor. When they are done, Maman returns and sits next to me.

"Are you feeling sick?" I ask. "You want me to get you some water?"

She shakes her head. "I should be the one asking you those questions. Let's go."

On the bus ride back my mother is still quiet, still playing with her rosary.

"Do you know how this rosary broke?" she asks.
"No."

"It was my birthday, May eighteenth, National Flag Day in Haiti, and my father had taken me to church. I was happy that for once he wasn't drunk. He bought me the rosary and took me to his friends all around Port-au-Prince, saying how lucky he was to have such a beautiful sixteen-year-old daughter. But before night my father was drunk again. I was serving him his meal when he broke the rosary from my neck, accusing me of cheating on him. The problem was I looked too much like my mother. I had hated her, too, for running off. He smashed the plate on the floor, then took this Haitian flag that was hanging on the wall. He wrapped himself in the old colors of the flag, red and black, then took his bottles of whiskey and rum and ran out into a rowdy passing *rara* group on the street."

The bus creeps along with the traffic on Flatbush Avenue.

Then after a moment, "You know, Mardi, I never want anything bad to happen to you. How could I? I'm your mother. Take what you need from me. I'll give you anything I have. Doing that is as easy for me as breathing. I have had experiences, many, and they have given me an extra eye you can't see."

She takes Papa's red handkerchief from me again to wipe her eyes.

"My God, this is horrible. . . . A horrible thing happened to you, a little innocent . . . but bad things happen to good people sometimes. I cannot explain why. The sun will burn itself out before I'll find an answer. I wish you could have given me this weight, all of it, to carry. . . ." She takes a deep breath and wraps my arm in hers. "Let's go home."

The house is empty when we get there. I feel like my mother and I are the last people left in Brooklyn. The last time I remember being alone with her was in Port-au-Prince. The whole family was planning a day trip somewhere and I got sick from eating too many sour tamarinds. She had stayed with me even though I threw up on her dress and shoes.

Maman goes into the kitchen to prepare food for a baptism this weekend and I go to the bedroom. I shut the door. The posters of Jean-Claude Van Damme, Reggie Miller, and Michael Jordan are there smiling, happy to see me. I stand in the middle of the room, looking around like a stranger, having the same sick feeling I had when I threw up on Maman. I see all the scenes from the cornfield in my head.

Hold.

Let go.

Bad.

Angry . . . angry . . .

Everything is gushing around. I reach inside my book bag and take out my pencil sharpener. I undo the screws, holding the small blade close to my wrist, ready to begin peeling because I don't have anywhere to go with these memories.

"Mardi," my mother calls from the kitchen. "Come. I've made you some tea."

I look at the door like my mother is standing there.

"Mardi!" she calls again after a while. "Mardi! Are you coming?" Now Jean-Claude, Reggie, and Michael stare at me, wondering what I will do.

Yes, Mardi, what will you do?

Breathe. . . .

What I think?

I think maybe the cornfields will never leave me.

"Mardi!" my mother shouts again. "I want you in front of me, now!"

"Yes!" I answer. "I'm coming!" On my way to the kitchen I stop at the bathroom. I wrap the blade in wet tissue and flush.

My mother and father go with me for the test results. Marisol takes us to a small room and leaves to get my file. I'm thinking maybe I shouldn't have said anything. Everyone in my house, except my uncle and aunt, looks at me funny now; I catch them staring at me like I'm someone they used to know. It's not a bad look, it's . . . funny. Like they're wondering about me and making up stories in their head.

The house is quieter. All conversations stop when I enter a room. Even when we found out Serina got a scholarship to the nursing college program she applied to, everyone tried not to be too happy. I teased Serina, saying that she got in because of my college essay, and to my surprise she agreed with me.

Grandmère sits up at night to watch me sleep. I've woken up a few times during the night to find her across the room with one small lamp lit. She couldn't see that I was awake. Sometimes I'd make a sound on purpose and she'd move to get up. Grandmère, Grandmère, yes, I know you're there.

I sit between my mother and father, directly facing a big framed poster of a smiling pregnant woman. She must want her baby. People in pictures always do.

My mother plays with her broken rosary and my father with his keys. I notice their hands, wrinkled. Maman's are chocolate and Papa's are pine wood–colored. Papa has a deep cut across his right palm and Maman a patch of white skin near her left thumb. They don't wear wedding rings anymore because they keep losing them.

"Henri, please!" my mother says. "Put those keys away."

Papa puts the keys in his pocket, then crosses his arms. "That doctor's been gone a while now."

Seven minutes.

"Maybe they've lost Mardi's file," Maman says.

Marisol comes back with my folder and takes the seat across from us. She opens my file. We lean toward her.

"The tests all came back negative," says Marisol. "Mardi doesn't have the HIV virus in her, nor any other sexually transmitted diseases. As far as these tests show, you are physically healthy."

My mother and I grab each other's hand. My father touches my knee. He keeps saying "God is good" in Créole. *"Bondye bon. Bondye bon."*

Marisol nods in agreement, looking right at me.

$\bullet \quad \bullet \quad \bullet$

I'm listening to tape number three of six tapes from the clinic. It's about sexual violence and abuse and all that sort of thing. I hear girls and women crying and telling their sad stories. Once a week I go to this class now where I meet people like that, people like me. I don't say a word when I'm there. I just listen.

I'm sitting on a chair in my father's reusable-things yard. It's cold but my mother gave me this long wool coat with a hood that has fur inside it. She knows I come here a lot and these last days of winter won't stop me.

I turn the tape off and open my book bag to write in Malice. Grandmère's sweets fall right out. I find them in my bag every now and then.

Malice is almost full. I write what I see: behind me the yard and the sky, and in front of me gates to the streets. Serina and my father are in the one-room wooden office by the gate. I can see them through the window, talking, looking at me, and drinking hot *kakaro*. Serina picked me up from school again today.

"Mardi!" My father opens the door and yells. "Aren't you hungry? What can I get for you?"

"Nothing!" I yell back. "We're fine, Papa!" Yes, Malice and I are fine.

My father nods. As he's about to close the office door, Pierre and Patrick come into the yard. Papa smiles, touches their shoulders, and gives them a bag of something. Pierre and Patrick walk up to me and I put Malice away.

"Hi, Mardi," they say.

"Hi."

"Aren't you cold sitting out here?" Patrick asks.

"No. I have a heavy coat on."

"Our toaster broke," says Pierre. "We came to pick up a piece from your father. Patrick's gonna try and fix it."

"Do you have to go back right away?" I ask.

"Not really," Pierre says.

"I was going to look for some things to finish my science report," I say. "Did you do yours?"

"I haven't even started," says Pierre. "Isn't Jilline your partner?"

"She's always busy."

"Patrick's helping me with mine."

"Yeah," Patrick says. "Pierre wants to do a volcano but that's too easy. I said we could do it on gravity and build something."

"You'll find a lot of things in my father's yard. You want to look?"

"Okay."

"Good idea."

Pierre, Patrick, and I stand on a small mountain, digging for things. I can see over the fence to across the street. There's a woman in front of the bakery who looks a lot like my mother: same height, hat, boots. After the three of us are done, the woman is still there. I decide to wave to the woman, and she waves back. She takes off her hat and I see her face; it is my mother.

I'm lying in my bed thinking about Santos. He's been saying hello to me lately, but I still see him around Mildred Rodriguez. Jilline told me Mildred is taking birth control pills. She had finally come over to work on the solar house for the science report. Jilline did type the report like she promised, but I'd nearly finished the house by then. All we were doing was painting it and adding clear plastic paper for the roof and windows. Everyone at home said it was really pretty and they could see themselves living in it. If I had done the house on paper, I'd tape it up on our front door.

"So how do you know for sure Mildred is taking birth control pills?" I asked Jilline, painting a side sky-blue.

"I just know, okay?"

"How old is Mildred? Fourteen? Fifteen?" What doctor would give her pills? When I went to the clinic, they had my mother sign all these permission forms before they could touch me.

"I think she's fifteen. I heard her mother gives them to her."

"Really? That's not true!"

"Trust me, Mardi, Mildred is on the pill. Do you even really know what birth control pills are and why people use them?"

"Yes, Jilline, of course I know! I'm not a little child!"

"All right, all right. Don't get all huffy on me. I'm just asking 'cause I know you don't have no TV and they keep you locked up."

"You can't learn everything from TV. I'm not as dumb as you think." What could backward Mardi, arriving here in a wooden boat from the monkey islands, know about anything? Mardi, from the poorest country in the Western Hemisphere—what could I possibly know?

"I wasn't calling you stupid. Look, just forget it. Do you want the trim on the window to be blue or pink? I think it should be hot pink."

My part was done. I didn't care what she did. She felt it and we worked in silence.

Anyhow, I'm lying in my bed tonight thinking about Santos. Yes, do I think he likes me. He blew me kisses, right? He kind of talks to me, doesn't he? I was standing in the school hallway today when I heard him saying to some other boys that he and Mildred were going back and forth but they were going to break up for sure this time because Mildred's been acting stupid. He also said he's looking for a new girlfriend. All I want from Santos is to hold hands. If not that, if I could just see him every day and have him smile at me, I'd be satisfied. And it's my turn. I need to tell him about me.

The next day at school my palms are sweaty. I'm holding a note for Santos in my hand.

Dear Santos,

You are the cutest boy in the whole school and possibly the entire world. I'd like to go out with you but my hair isn't long enough for me to throw down so you could climb into my room (it's not really my room, I share it with my grandmother, sister, and aunt—who you know). I won't tell you who I am because I am scared. Keep your eyes open. I don't even blink when I look at you.

Tuesday

P.S. If you speak French, you'll know who I am.

I wrote the letter on Serina's nice paper and sprayed it with her expensive perfume, the one that smells like a vanilla rose crushed in a book.

Right before lunch I go to the bathroom and hide in the stairwell for a few minutes to make sure no one's in the hallway. My heart's pounding like an African drum. I close my eyes and listen.

Calm yourself, Mardi. It's not like you're on a cliff about to jump off.

I don't know how long I stay in the stairwell. When I'm ready, I hurry out and tuck the letter on the side of Santos's locker. I hide behind a row of lockers not too far down. I wait for him to come out of his math class. I should run but I want to see his face when he sees my letter.

But here comes Mildred Rodriguez down the hall like she's everything beautiful. Please. She's as skinny as a giraffe but walks like a rhino in heat. Mildred stops in front of Santos's locker. I run back to the stairwell. I open the stairwell door a crack to see what she's doing.

She's reading my letter!

Mildred laughs and crumples it up. "Yeah, right," she says. She tears a page from her spiral notebook, folds it, and puts it where my letter was.

When she leaves, I go back to Santos's locker and read her note. There's a perforated line to tear along so the page won't have ragged edges from the spiral binding. If I had a boyfriend like Santos, I would take the time to tear along the dotted line. I hear people say that God is in the details. Then the devil must be in the ragged edges of letters that look like rats have bitten them. Mildred Rodriguez may be pretty, but I can tell she knows nothing about the finer points of romance. Her note says:

Come to my house after school.
My mother won't be home.

Wow. Is that all she needs to write for Santos and other boys to go to her? I rip up Mildred's note and stuff it in my pocket. I'll flush it down the toilet later. I take out my second letter—a backup. As I hold letter number two in my hand, doubt, as Grandmère would say, taps my shoulder. Should I leave it? Maybe it was good that Mildred took my first letter. And when Santos guesses it's me? What if he laughs? What if he throws it away like Mildred did?

I leave the letter anyway.

"I'll share a secret with you," Serina says to me one day when I'm helping her clean and season fish for the Sunday meal. "Remember that condom Maman found under my bed the day after the Christmas dance?"

"Yeah?"

"It was really mine. Uncle Perrin was covering up for me." Serina has stars in her eyes like she's telling me she's just discovered gold.

"That was months ago. Why are you telling me this now?"

She shrugs. "I thought you'd like to know."

"I already know."

"Oh." She's quiet for a few moments, then she starts: "That boy is cute."

"Who?"

"The one at the supermarket where Matant Widza works."

"She told you?"

"No, she didn't have to. What's his name? Sanchez?"

"Santos. And don't tell anyone."

"Oh yes, Santos. Of course I won't tell anyone. He seems nice. Very friendly. I don't know why Aunt Widza doesn't like him. I went in there the other day and he asked me about you."

I drop a fish head on the floor but keep my cool. "Oh, really?"

"Well," Serina says, "he came up to me and told me the two of you were in the same school. I think he likes you."

"No he doesn't."

"If people ask for you, you either owe them something or they like you," she says.

I hide my smile from Serina. I would never be sad again if I could believe what she's saying.

Uncle Perrin pops into the kitchen, dangling a set of keys in his hand.

"You two ladies need to look at this." He puts his hands on our shoulders, leading us to the window.

"It's a nice garbage truck," I say. That's all I can see down on the street.

"Ha, ha, Mardi, *la petite comédienne*," Uncle Perrin says. "The truck is blocking it."

When the truck pulls away, we see a small red car with a dent in the door.

"Is it yours?" Serina asks.

"Yep."

"Can it move?" I ask.

Serina laughs.

"You've only been working two months and you already have a car?" I ask.

"I plan, I save, I accomplish," Uncle Perrin says. "My supervisor at work sold it to me for a few hundred dollars. I just picked it up."

"Can we go see Pélé?" I ask.

"Pélé has soccer practice on Saturdays," Uncle Perrin says.

"Can I drive it?" Serina asks. "I have my license."

"But no driving experience," says my uncle. "I'll take you for a drive. Let's go."

"We're cleaning fish," I say.

"We'll put the fish in the refrigerator until we get back." Serina throws her apron off. "Can we pick up a friend?"

"Will we be gone long?" I ask.

"Twenty minutes."

But we're gone for hours. Uncle Perrin drives us all over Brooklyn. I sit next to him while Serina is in the back with her "friend," Jean-Robert.

Spring is just beginning and it's still cold, but we have all the windows down, our heads and hands sticking out, the wind doing a merry-go-round inside the car. I feel the car floating. It's good to be moving.

We stop at Coney Island, where there's hardly anyone on the boardwalk or the rides and almost all the stores are closed. We eat hot dogs—Jean-Robert insists that he pay for everyone and Serina smiles at him proudly. Afterward, she and Jean-Robert walk barefoot on the beach, giggling. I imagine it's Santos and me out there, holding hands,

197

kissing a little, testing the water with our toes, then backing away as if we've touched electricity.

Uncle Perrin and I sit on a bench facing the ocean. "This is nice," I say. "I've never been here before. Can we come back in the summer?"

"Yes," he answers, but his attention is on the water and not with me.

"Is there something out there?" I ask after a few minutes.

"There's always something out there, the survivors trying to cross."

I wait a few minutes more. "Monnonk, why don't you ever talk about the camps in Guantánamo?"

"The same reason you never talked about what happened to you," he snaps.

I turn numb with hurt and embarrassment. I should know better than to pick at him. "*Eskize-m,* Monnonk. I'm sorry." I never want to upset him again.

"No, Mardi, don't be. I don't mean to snap at you. It's automatic to think of boats when you look at the ocean. It's life and death, that water. If my life were a boat, there'd be tons of people on it in the middle of the ocean, screaming to get off. I thought I was my own captain, I thought I built a good boat, but . . . Oh, I don't know, I don't know. . . . Enough of this. I'm here now, right?"

I nod and he smiles at me like before. Jean-Robert is about to dump a laughing Serina in the water. Uncle Perrin hurries over to them yelling, *"Fètatansyon!"* Be careful.

I look out far into the ocean. "I'm here, too," I whisper. "I'm here, too."

Ike bites his lower lip as he walks pass my desk in history class.

"Hey, sex."

He's in early today, smelling like someone poured rum on his shirt. He sings a soft lullaby so no one but me can hear: "Rock-a-my Mardi on the treetop, when Ike comes the cradle will drop, and down will come Mardi, cradle and all. . . ." Then out loud he says, "What, you don't like my song, sweet tits?"

"She ain't sweet and she ain't got no tits," laugh some kids next to me.

"I think I'ma sit here next to my pal." Ike sits across from me. "It's lonely all the way over there where I am." The boy whose desk Ike is sitting in is about to walk down the aisle to his seat. When the boy sees Ike, he changes direction and goes somewhere else. I was hoping he would fight for his seat.

"Leave me alone, Ike." I say this more to myself than to him.

"What did you say?" He leans so close his breath burns my face. The bell rings and the teacher walks in, telling everyone to take their seats, but Ike stays put.

I look straight ahead, heart drumming. I'm so tired of this. I grit my teeth. "Leave–me–a–lone."

"Sweet tits . . . ," he keeps on saying.

"BACK OFF, *ISAAC*, AND LEAVE ME ALONE!" I take my history textbook and throw it on the floor.

Everyone freezes. In the silence I feel myself growing.

I expect Ike to grab my throat or threaten to kill me after school. But he starts to laugh, like he's heard a good joke.

"Well, now, Mardi, damn. Who woulda thought?" He winks at me, then goes back to his own seat.

At lunchtime everyone is talking:

". . . She told Ike to stop messing with her. . . ."

". . . She said she was gonna beat him up after school. . . ."

". . . and Ike got all scared and ran out the room. . . ."

Let them talk. I don't care. I sit at my usual empty table and open the book I'm reading for the third time, *Are You There, God? It's Me, Margaret.*

Someone taps me on the shoulder. I turn around, annoyed because I'm in the middle of my favorite chapter.

"What!"

It's Santos, and I jump back.

"Hey, chicken, don't tell me you afraid of little ol' me now?"

I look at the floor, making believe I just lost something. "Just wanted to say hi."

"Hi."

"Bye."

"Bye."

But Santos doesn't leave. "I won't go until you look at me."

I grab Malice and write: *Don't melt. Don't melt, Mardi.*

"You like your book more than you like me?"

I put my pen down and slowly look up into his face. I stay together but I'm completely dumb now.

"You know, me and Mildred, we're breaking."

"What are you going to break?"

"Us. Our relationship."

"Oh!"

"Yeah . . . Well, I gotta go. See you around." I watch him walk out of the lunchroom. I open Malice: *Okay to breathe.*

Later in science class I get more good news: Jilline and I win first prize for our report on solar energy! I was right! Half of the students made the same plaster volcanoes, and the other half, including Pierre, who won third prize, only had their papers to turn in. We were the only ones to think of the sun and build a house. We get to go away to a summer camp upstate for free! It's a science camp and we'll get to study the Earth, but the brochure also says I'll learn how to swim, take painting classes, hike in the mountains—do all those things I read about in books.

"So what?" Jilline says. "We get to go to camp. Big deal."

"I haven't been away from Flatbush since I got here."

"You've never been anywhere. I guess I shouldn't be surprised you want to go. All little kids wanna go away to camp and leave their mommies and daddies."

"I'm not a little kid."

"You know what I mean."

"No I don't. I don't understand you anymore, Jilline. Sometimes I think you say things just to make me feel I'm under you."

"You're so sensitive, Mardi."

"I am when you treat me like I just fell off a boat. I need to go away, but you don't have to go to camp if you don't want."

"Damn right I don't have to! I got a cutie and a car waiting for me in South Carolina. I'm gonna have some real fun. Aren't you jealous?" Jilline pretends she's playing, but it's easy to see she enjoys being better than me.

What I think?

I think maybe she's always been this way and I'm just now noticing it.

"No," I say, "I'm not jealous of you at all."

"Yeah, right."

"How can I be jealous of someone who doesn't have a mother and father?" I shock the high-and-mighty out of her.

"You dumb-ass chickenhead!" she says. "I don't need a mother and father to know who I am. I've got my own room, my own TV, stereo, money, all the clothes I want and no a-dult bothering me telling me what to do!"

"I know," I tell her. "That's what your problem is." And with that I turn on her and walk away.

That night I show everyone the certificate I got for the report. Uncle Perrin hugs me and spins me around while Aunt Widza claps. I tape the certificate on the front door.

"Good for you," Maman says.

"Aaahhh," begins Grandmère, "don't you get some money or at least a trophy? For your hard work all they give you is a piece of paper?"

"No," I answer. "I do get something else. I get to go to a science camp for free in upstate New York. I'll learn about the Earth. It'll be good for my education."

"You should have a lot of fun," says Serina.

Maman and Papa are quiet and look at each other.

"I don't know," my mother says. "I don't like my children far from me."

"Haiti is far," Aunt Widza points out.

"It's not the same thing," my father says. "Mardi was with family, not strangers."

"What about the Saint Joseph's summer program right here?" Maman suggests. "Pierre's father tells me he sends Pierre there every year and she always has a good time. Even Patrick will be going there this summer."

"I want to be in a place where there's a lot of trees," I say.

"Yes, go to the trees," says Aunt Widza.

"It's a nice idea, and we're happy you worked hard and earned the prize, but . . ." Papa doesn't finish.

I leave the kitchen and go into the bathroom. I open the window, letting the chill air cool me down. They do want me to live in a box for the rest of my life! What would they do if I jumped out the window? Yes, they'd be sorry. An ambulance would have to come get me and Maman and Papa would have to pay all this money for the hospital bill. Yes, that would get them upset. But all I do is stick my head and arms out the window, trying to hold on to the wind.

There's a knock at the door. I know it's Uncle Perrin because he's the only one who knocks in this house. *"Oui?"* I lower the window and sit on the toilet seat lid. It's Aunt Widza. She sits on the edge of the bathtub but doesn't say anything.

She stares at me. I stare back at her. Then she gets up and tiptoes out like a mouse. Oh, please! If you're going to interrupt me, at least say something!

For the next few days I'm sour-faced. I make sure Maman and Papa see me. The very least they can do is the most they can do, let me go already! But I don't want them to send me out of guilt over what happened to me in the cornfields. I want them to let me go only because I've asked them.

Uncle Perrin and Serina must have spoken to them because they start asking me things like how far is the place, what kind of security would it have, and would they be able to come get me if they wanted.

One night I wake up to go to the bathroom and find my grandmother at the kitchen table with a candle and a cup of tea. I slide into the chair across from her.

"Aaahhh, Mardi," she sighs. "Can't sleep, either?"

"I want to go to camp, Grandmère."

"Yes, I know. I've spoken to them, too. Don't worry. You're going."

"Really?"

"I'm almost sure."

"Almost?"

"Aaahhh." She leans closer. "Can you keep a secret?"

I lean closer, too.

"They told me you'll go."

"Yes! Yes! Yes!"

"Shhhhh, quiet."

"Then, Grandmère, why don't they just say it? Why keep me waiting?"

"You don't just send your child off without thinking about it. And it's in the waiting you get to appreciate the answer and realize what you have and don't have. Did I ever tell you the story about Malice and Bouki and the days Bouki kept waiting eight days for the next Tuesday?"

"I already know it. Bouki is dumb enough to fall for Malice's tricks and ends up tied to a tree forever."

"You only know half the story. Bouki did wait a long time. But his tears were so precious and sincere they went through the dry earth and gave new life to the barren tree he was tied to. The tree grew golden leaves and mangos. It was so thankful it let Bouki go with sacks and sacks of gold fruit. When Malice saw Bouki with his riches, he couldn't believe it. 'I thought I'd never see you again,' he cried.

" 'I must thank you, my friend,' Bouki said to him. 'Because of you I know how well I'll be living all the Tuesdays of my life!' "

Grandmère pats my hand. She gets up, touches my shoulder, and leaves the kitchen. The next day my mother says I needed a suitcase, and my father says he'll have to fix the van for the long drive upstate.

The perfect day for the annual class trip to a farm in New Jersey is this sunny morning. The yellow bus we're on takes a curve and makes everyone move with it. We've been on the bus about an hour. I look over at Pierre, asleep next to me. Her mouth is open and there's dried saliva at the corners of her lips. She looks like she's making that awful face on purpose. I put my hand over my mouth to keep from laughing.

I lean back to fall asleep when the bus arrives. There's trees and grass everywhere. This is what it'll be like next week when I go to summer camp. Everyone wakes up and starts clapping and cheering.

"Now, now, settle down," Mrs. Orlando tells us as we get our things from under the seats. "Let me just run down the schedule. We'll have small group tours of the place. If you want to roam on your own don't go beyond the red fences around the area, and we'll meet back here for lunch at noon. Got that?"

Everyone mutters "yeah" and almost knocks her down trying to get off the bus. You'd think the gates were opening and we were being let out of prison.

I watch Santos with his arm around Mildred. Didn't he say they were breaking up? They're walking off together down a dirt path. Santos is whispering something in her ear, and at first she giggles, shaking her head. He whispers something again that takes her smile away. She pushes him and angrily walks down the path. He follows her.

"Let that one go." Jilline walks up behind me. "You never gonna have him." She's still mad at me for reminding her that she doesn't have a mother or father. I know it was mean of me and I told her I was sorry, but she wanted to stay angry.

Just then the zipper in her bag breaks and all her things scatter on the ground. I pick up her lipstick and Pierre gets her bikini, and we hand them back to her. She grabs them, rushing off without saying thank you.

"Come on," Pierre says, "let's go to the horse stables first. I wanna–"

"I just want to walk around by myself," I tell her.

"Okay. Don't get lost. I'll see you at lunchtime."

I go down the same dirt path Santos and Mildred were on. I see their sneaker prints in the soft ground and squash them with my sandals. Their prints lead off the path between two bushes. I keep going straight.

I come to a stream that, according to the map they gave us, leads to a pond farther down. This farm is a historic site because some general from the Revolutionary War lived here or something like that. I visit the famous war cannon—which is directly in front of a tree—and then there's the historic log cabin where they say George Washington once slept. The cabin is all boarded up and not much bigger than the wooden shed in my grandmother's backyard. At one point a flock of birds dip in the air and almost fly into me. They get so close I feel the fresh wind their wings make.

When I get tired, I head back to the stream and rest near the pond under a tree that looks like the leaves have a cold, all limp with bent-over branches. I think this is a weeping willow. Aunt Widza says even trees cry.

I eat my cheese-and-crackers snack and watch the reflection of the world on the water. The picture there is so much softer.

It's quiet here, and it smells so good. I open my bag and take out the rocks I used to put in my bed. One by one I throw them in the pond.

I look down at my hands and rub them together, liking the feel of them. I lift my skirt and touch my legs. My skin is smooth, not broken. I touch my face. My eyes are big, my nose is wide, and my lips are smiling.

A mama duck crosses the pond, her babies following. She leads without looking back, like nothing can ever happen to her duckies. I take out Malice and write: *I am God for today and this is my world.* Then, out of nowhere, a rock lands in the water right by one of her babies and the mama duck goes crazy.

I turn around. Santos is on a small hill above me. He

throws another rock in the water, then comes down to the willow tree. He doesn't say anything but looks at me the same way he did in the lunchroom. I start to feel hot and embarrassed.

"You having a good time?" he asks.

"Y-yes."

"Good." He gives me a quick smile and looks around him. "This is a quiet spot. No one's around. We're all by ourselves now."

The moment he says this, a light switch goes on inside me.

I slowly get up.

"You got prettier this year," he says, with one hand in his pocket. "You look a lot like your aunt. You know, Tuesday's my favorite day of the week." He pulls my letter out and shows it to me. "But if you want to be my girlfriend . . ."

He tries to kiss me but I turn my head just in time for his kiss to land on my cheek. I push him away.

"Don't act like you ain't been waiting for this moment. Why you write me the letter, then?"

"I–I thought you liked me. . . . Y-you looked at me and you winked. . . ."

His eyes are narrow, the color of hot grease, and I can hear his thoughts sizzling. I know I'm being fried in it.

"I'm going back to the bus." I take some steps back but trip and land in the pond. Santos rolls his eyes and says very seriously, "Come here!"

Like I'm his.

I get up dripping and laughing. I don't belong to anybody except me. I take Santos's arm and pull him into the pond, too, and splash him.

"What you doing?" he yells.

I keep splashing.

"Yo! I said—"

Keep splashing.

"You crazy—"

"Santos! Santos! Santos! If you shut up and cool off now, maybe I could still like you!" He tries to get me with the water but my splashing is fiercer than his. I plan to empty the pond on him even if he is the best-looking boy in Flatbush.

Santos covers his face and climbs back over the hill. I get out of the pond and pick up the letter I wrote Santos. I tear it into pieces and let the wind keep it.

I walk up the path toward the bus. Ike and some of his friends are sitting at a wooden table off to the side. They've got their radio, music, and smoke. Ike sees me and turns my way. I face him, the space between us enough for three cars.

That's the way I like it. I keep walking.

My suitcase is almost ready.

"Mardi's taking too many things," says my mother. She should talk. She's the one who bought me this big suitcase filled with shorts, skirts, and summer dresses.

"Will Mardi have a chance to wear all these clothes?" My father is sitting on the suitcase, trying to close it. "This is going to pop open."

"Don't crush the lamp I gave her," says Aunt Widza.

"Yes, and make sure the shampoo and conditioner don't leak," Serina says.

"What about the *dous* and bread I made? Will the sweet potato pie fit?" Grandmère is holding a bag full of bread and a plastic container wrapped in aluminum foil.

"Let Mardi carry the food," says Uncle Perrin. "Wait! See if these books will fit in that space."

"Anything Mardi is missing we'll bring to her on parents' day."

"Oh! I'll have to call and make sure Pélé can come with us."

"I swear this suitcase is going to bust."

"It can bust, but not the lamp."

"Maybe I should make more bread?"

"Grandmère, I'm sure there's bread wherever Mardi is going."

My family is funny. I'm standing right in front of them and as usual they go on as if I'm not there. But I know they know I'm here.

It's two o'clock in the morning and I can't sleep.

There's news that Haiti's president might return to the country. If he does, Grandmère and Aunt Widza will go home. Uncle Perrin is staying either way.

I'm thinking about it all in my bed. I'll be going away to camp in a few hours. I play with my mother's rosary, the broken one she had fixed and gave me.

I'm thirsty.

I hang my rosary on a nail by my pillow and get out of bed. I tiptoe to the kitchen and pour a glass of lemonade. Grandmère makes the best lemonade.

I'm at the kitchen table. The moon, or maybe the tall streetlamps, barely lights the room. From where I sit I can see the outline of Uncle Perrin's guitar leaning against the wall. I hear Monnonk snoring softly in the living room. What a wonderful sound it is.

The window is wide open because it's hot. Below I hear the Flatbush street symphony: an occasional car whizzing by, pumping some loud beat.

I look around the kitchen. In the dark my eyes can still recognize the big cooking spoons, the I LOVE HAITI wooden machete souvenir, the local bodega calendar of a topless woman, the three pictures of fruits, the floral plastic tablecloth, toaster, blender, Brillo, Palmolive, and the patchwork-quilt rag that hangs on the refrigerator door. I have good eyes. I can even see the fading crack on the wall in the shape of Hispaniola.

What I think?

I think I will be all right.

Because I am good.

Still.

AUTHOR'S NOTE

In 1991, Haiti was all over the news. A coup d'état caused widespread bloodshed and violence and a massive exodus from the country. Lives were uprooted and changed forever. Many would agree that these were the island's darkest days.

I was born and raised in New York City, and this was really the first time events from my mother's and father's birthplace touched me. I was shaken by it all, especially by the horrifying stories of sexual violence against women and children. Maybe it was because I was a young woman myself, living safely in the United States, and couldn't conceive of my life being torn from its hinges. How would one survive such a tragedy? The question was the seed for this story, and I have tried my best to answer it with this book.

ACKNOWLEDGMENTS

I cannot take full responsibility for having the strength, insight, and courage to write this story. Many share in this beautiful weight for their past and present nurturing and loving support:

My family, for the richness of memories they give me: my father Beliotte, sister Ti Sè (a.k.a. Marie), brother Jean Kopa *Play*-cide, Matant Carmelite, Nènèl, Raymonde, Horlna, Holny, Ti Hogarth, and Mama (a.k.a. Marjorie).

Fred Hudson and the Frederick Douglass Creative Arts Center (believers #1) for the DorisJean Austin Fellowship and the Frederick Douglass Fellowship for Young African American Fiction Writers.

Marie Brown, my agent (believer #2).

Wendy Lamb, my great editor and true fan (believer #3).

Grosvenor Neighborhood House, a very valuable space in my early adolescence.

Lenny Fraser, Martin Simmons, Wendy Guity, John Lucero, Frank Mason, Brian "B.A." Wright, Indra Chaitoo, Indira Chaitoo, Matant Ismela L'Amour, Godfather "Manno" Josaphat, Celita Joseph, Charlemagne Davilmar, Yusuf Tafari, St. Gregory the Great church choir.

I thank God for you all!

ABOUT THE AUTHOR

Jaïra Placide was born in New York City and began writing at the age of twelve, when she wrote a play for her sixth-grade class to perform. She received her Bachelor of Fine Arts and Master of Fine Arts degrees in dramatic writing from New York University's Tisch School of the Arts. She works in children's book publishing and is currently writing a collection of short stories.

Fresh Girl is her first novel.